ALWAYS BY MY SIDE

TRINITY LAKES ROMANCE
BOOK FOUR

IOLA GOULTON

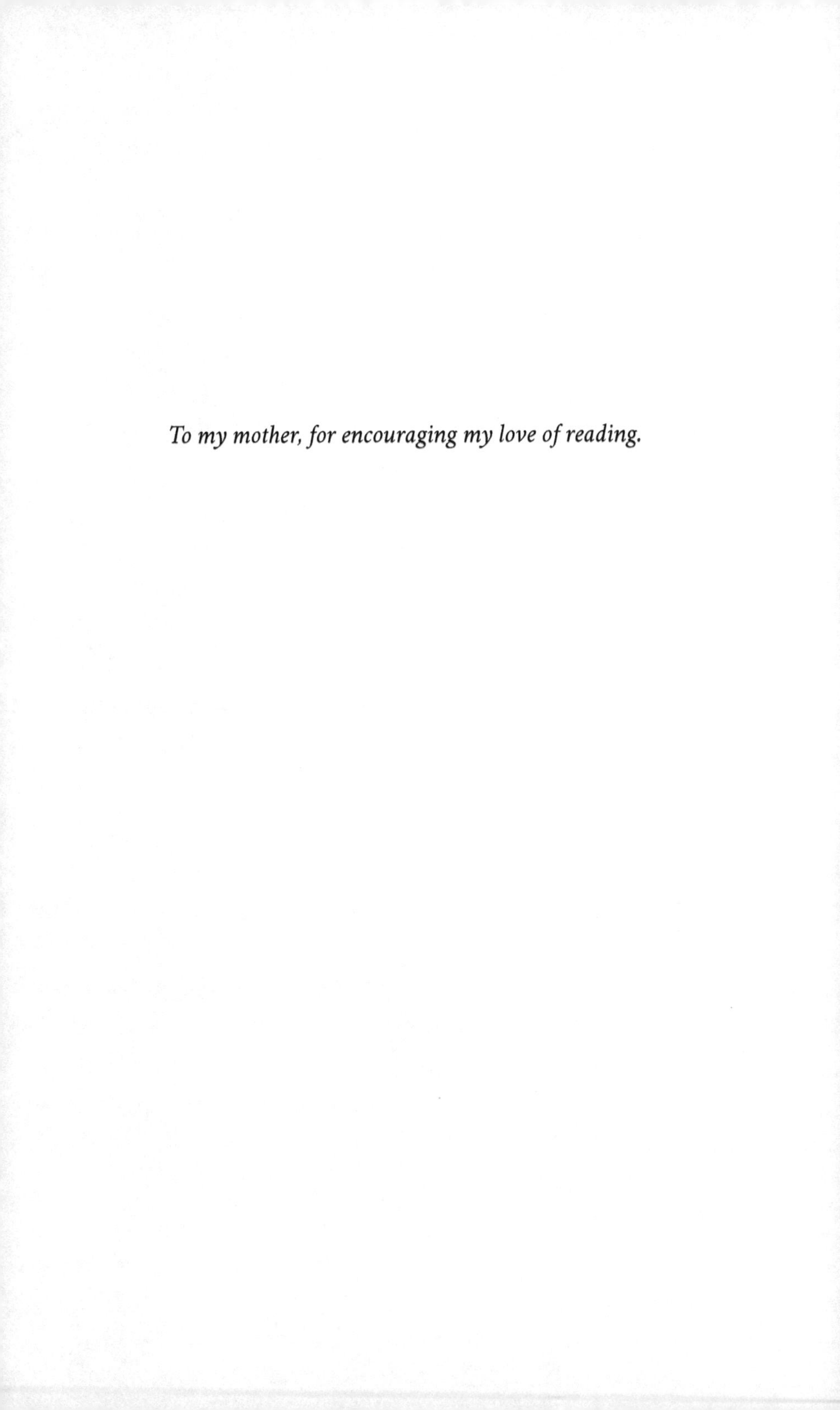

To my mother, for encouraging my love of reading.

Love God and do whatever you please: for the soul trained in love to God will do nothing to offend the One who is Beloved.
—St. Augustine

CHAPTER ONE

The last person Tabitha Thomas expected to walk in the front door of the Lakeview Inn on a brisk early spring afternoon was Logan Wylde. Logan, her brother's college roommate. Her sister's one-time plus-one. Her secret teenage crush, the man she hadn't mentally moved on from in four years. Yet here he was, complete with his killer looks, killer smile, and killer motorcycle. That explained the deep engine rumbling along the lakefront.

Dad appeared from the office off the foyer as though he'd been expecting Logan's arrival. "Logan, my boy. Good to see you."

"Good to be here," Logan said in his distinctive New Zealand accent. He gave Dad's hand a quick shake, then turned to Tabby. "Hope you're well, Tabitha. Good to see you."

"Hi, Logan. Come in."

Why was he here? And how long was he here for? Not long, hopefully. It was a lot easier to ignore and avoid a secret crush in another city, another country, than one staying in the same house. She stepped back and offered her hand. "Were we expecting you?" As manager, housekeeper, cook, and general gopher, she should know, but she was so busy she wouldn't know what day of the week it was if her smartphone didn't remind her.

"Your brother called last night after you'd gone to bed," Dad said.

Great. Couldn't Dad have warned her? Then she would have worn something more flattering than her grossest cleaning gear —the stained sweatshirt and holey sweatpants were not appropriate attire for anyone outside the family to see. Not that she wanted to impress Logan.

She didn't.

Not at all.

"Sorry for the late notice." Logan hefted his travel-worn backpack from his shoulders and leaned it against his leg. "My plans fell through, so I needed somewhere to stay for a couple of months. Trent said you'd be able to put me up."

For a couple of months? When he'd never stayed longer than a weekend before? She must have misheard him. Tabby took a deep breath.

"We don't have any vacant guest rooms at the moment." Which Dad knew, although Tiffy and Trent wouldn't.

"You're always welcome." Easy for Dad to say.

"Trent said I could bunk in his room." Typical Trent, making promises he didn't have to keep.

"Tabby, I'll leave you to show Logan upstairs, if you don't mind. "I have a call with Wayne Gilbertson about the country club."

About taxes, or trusts, or something Tabby didn't need or want to know about. She'd leave that to Dad.

"No problem," Logan said. "I know it's your busy season and you have lots to do."

And so did Tabby. Since Gran's death, Tabby had run the family B&B on her own. Dad was in the middle of tax season and didn't have time to help with the endless list of day-to-day tasks. His contribution was greeting midweek guests who arrived while she was at her afternoon job at Hannah Gilbertson's rowing club.

Tabby barely had time to cook, clean, and cater for their paying guests, let alone entertain Trent's freshman college roommate-turned-closest friend.

"Is Trent's room still the health hazard it was in his freshman year?" Logan was two years older than the triplets, so he'd been a junior the year he roomed with Trent.

"He was home for Gran's funeral, and I haven't had a chance to make it up since." The cleanliness of Trent's room wasn't the reason for her hesitation, but she took the excuse, even if the funeral had been two months ago. There was no way in Washington she'd admit to Logan—or her father—that she'd had a huge crush on Logan since they'd first met almost five years ago. "Let's go look."

"I'm sure it will be fine." Logan hefted his pack onto his right shoulder and picked up his helmet.

"Follow me." Tabby sighed and headed toward the family side of the inn, then waited at the bottom of the stairs that led to the family bedrooms.

She looked back to make sure Logan was following. He moved slowly, favoring his right leg. She looked again. That wasn't a motorcycle boot on his right foot. It was a walking boot.

"Is there something wrong with your foot?"

"Why I'm here, unfortunately. Hit a rock while snowboarding down an advanced run and twisted my ankle as I landed. Nothing broken, but it's a nasty sprain."

"Is it serious?" Tabby paused halfway up the stairs, waiting for Logan to catch up. Who knew where Logan had been snowboarding, but it couldn't have been anywhere nearby.

She might be trying not to care about Logan, but she could still care as a family friend, right? He'd visited often enough over the last four years to have been elevated from "guest" to "family friend" status, even if Dad treated him more like an actual member of the family. People cared about their friends. It was normal. Natural. Nice.

But spending time with Logan? She'd fall for him all over again, even knowing nothing could come of her crush. He was all wrong for her—an adventurer, a foreigner, and not a Christian.

"Nothing major. Just need to rest up and do the exercises the physio—sorry, you call them physical therapists—the exercises the PT gave me. No skiing, no hiking, no rock climbing."

Most of the reasons tourists visited Trinity Lakes in March. That left canoeing, kayaking, sailing, or fishing on Lake Wainscott or one of the connecting rivers, or endless rounds of golf —if he used a golf cart.

"I hope you don't get bored. Trinity's attractions are mostly the kind your doctor wants you to avoid."

"The doctor did give me that lecture." Logan continued climbing the stairs, right foot first then left.

"But didn't say anything about riding a motorcycle for how many hours to southern Washington with a sprained ankle?" Tabby paused at the top of the stairs to allow Logan time to catch up.

"I don't think she considered how I was traveling." He used the faux-innocent tone people used when telling a half-truth, like describing scrawny newborn babies as beautiful, or dry Thanksgiving turkey as tasty.

"Men." That was exactly the kind of thing Trent would have done in their teenage years. "What are your plans once you've recovered?"

"I've signed up as a camp counselor for the summer."

"At Camp Trinity?" She'd done a couple of seasons as camp counselor during high school and enjoyed the experience . . . and the spending money that came with it. The job came with free room and board and paid well enough for a teenager with no other source of income, but it wasn't a career role.

"Training starts in the middle of May." Logan met Tabby at the top of the stairs.

Spending a summer in the sun, leading laughing teens would be fun. But she couldn't. She had enough to do between running the inn, and cooking and baking for church, not to mention her afternoon job at the rowing club.

A job that started in twenty-three minutes, which meant she had exactly thirteen minutes to shower, change into her uniform, and head out the door for a ten-minute power walk to the rowing club.

And there was too much to do here at the inn, starting with decluttering, cleaning, and refurbishing Gran's suite. When she had the time. When she had the energy. When she could face the unwanted yet necessary project.

"You couldn't stay at the camp?"

"I asked, but they said I can't stay there until training starts. Something about insurance or liability."

So he was staying here. No surprises there. Logan was an adventurer, moving from one short-term dead-end job to another as he circumnavigated the globe multiple times a year. She tracked his travels through the dozens of postcards he'd sent Trent over the three years since Logan had graduated, postcards she'd rescued from the trash and pinned to her corkboard.

Tabby opened the door to Trent's room. It didn't smell, which was a start. She was used to it smelling somewhere between a high school locker room and a sewer. The floor was clear, and the covers were pulled up on both beds, although no one was bouncing any pennies on those sheets.

But there was a weeks-old half-full water glass on the bedside table, along with several screwed-up tissues and Trent's Bible. She scooped the tissues into the half-full trash can, replaced the Bible in the bookshelf, and picked up the glass.

And there was a photograph of Gran with the three of them, back when they were in grade school. She picked up the picture in her spare hand and hitched a breath at their three happy faces.

Logan limped into the room behind her, propped his backpack against the wall, balanced his helmet on top, and sat on the bed.

"It doesn't smell. I call that a win."

"I'll check the bathroom and bring you some clean towels." She was going to be late for work. She'd shoot Hannah a text.

Logan crossed the room and opened the door to the en suite. "Bathroom looks clean. Towels would be great. Thank you."

Tabby popped her head around the en suite door. "It's not the disaster I thought it might be." Sure, it wasn't cleaned to Gran's standards, but there was no dirty laundry on the floor and no visible grime or mold. Not that the seventies-era brown showed grime or mold or any other hygiene sins.

"I'll be back in a minute. She left the bedroom, leaving the door behind her ajar, pulled out her phone, and shot Hannah a quick text.

Going to be maybe 15 mins late. Unexpected houseguest. Sorry and thanks for understanding.

Hannah wouldn't mind. Tabby would have to eat when she got to work—there should be some chocolate chip cookies in the rowing club kitchen. Hannah's Granny Gracie had brought in a batch just yesterday. She liked to keep "her girls" fed, knowing it wasn't good to be hangry when dealing with paying customers. Tabby felt more than a little hangry now.

Goodness. Two months in the same house as Logan Wylde. Wylde by name and wild by nature, if even half Trent's tales over the years were true. Maybe sharing a house would finally cure her crush. After all, Logan was the wrong kind of man for her.

Yet there was something compelling about Logan Wylde. Maybe it was the cute Kiwi accent that left her wanting to hear more. Maybe it was the way his cornflower-blue eyes seared her soul when he looked at her. Maybe it was the tanned skin and blond Heath Ledger corkscrew curls that left her breathless, as if she'd just hiked up Mt. St. Helens.

Maybe it was the person she wished he would become.

———

LOGAN LAY BACK on the bed as Tabitha left the room and closed the door. His ankle ached, and it was past time to take the doctor's advice to RICE—rest, ice, compress, and elevate.

This wasn't what he'd planned. He'd planned to spend the next eight weeks on a personal pilgrimage, backpacking through Portugal and Spain, but he couldn't walk twenty-plus kilometers a day on a munted ankle. And he had no interest in hanging around in Banff with no job, no friends, and no purpose. So he'd accepted Trent's invitation and traveled to Trinity.

But it had been a long motorcycle ride from Banff, he was tired, and his ankle ached after the ten-hour motorcycle ride and international border crossing. The roads had been narrower and windier and bumpier once he got off the inter-state, which meant he'd had to ride more carefully to avoid jarring his ankle . . . which was a lot more painful than he'd let on to Tabitha.

But he was here now. He closed his eyes, grateful he had a place to stay. Grateful he was covered under his dad's medical insurance policy for another six months. Grateful he'd arrived safely. Grateful he had his next job lined up, even if it didn't start for another two months. That should give his ankle time to heal.

Please God, let that be long enough.

The last time he'd twisted this ankle, it had taken four months to heal enough to run on it—too long. He'd lost his place in rookie camp, and with that, his career in football.

Footsteps sounded on the wooden floors outside the room, so he opened his eyes and sat up. Tabitha came in with an armload of linen.

"I've brought you clean sheets as well, just in case."

"Great." Logan swung his legs off the bed and pulled back the sheets. Wrinkled. Who knew who had slept here last. Possibly him, although he hadn't visited since Thanksgiving. "Yeah, I'll take those sheets. Thanks." The linen smelled of mountain air and sunshine.

"Let me," Tabitha said.

"No, I can do it," Logan said. "I appreciate you offering me a place to stay. The least I can do is make my own bed and help around the place."

"Thank you." Her tone was perfunctory, as though his offering was a simple courtesy, not an actual promise. "If you don't mind, I'm going to shoot off. I'm running late for work. Just leave the dirty sheets in the hallway, and I'll pick them up later."

"Work? I thought running this place was a full-time job, especially now . . ." Now her grandmother had died. Tabitha had always been the triplet who was closest to Martha, who'd died in January. Trent had told Logan Tabitha was taking the loss hard.

"I work weekday afternoons at Hannah Gilbertson's rowing club," Tabitha said. "I'll fill you in later. I must run."

"Sure. Have a good afternoon," Logan said. Was she going to be late because of him? He hoped not.

He was tired, but Tabitha looked beyond tired. Grief? Too

much work? Not sleeping enough? He didn't know and couldn't tell. What he could do was not add to her burdens. Instead, he could clean bathrooms and manage laundry and generally be available to greet guests or do whatever other jobs needed doing to run a three-room bed-and-breakfast in a small tourist town.

Logan bowed his head, weary. "Lord, thank You for bringing me here, for providing me with a place to stay. I don't know why I'm here two months before I'd planned to be, but You know so I guess I'll figure it out. I'm grateful I can stay here."

He had no idea where he would have gone if it wasn't for Trent's offer.

"Lord, Tabitha looks tired. I guess she's still grieving her grandmother. It's only been a couple of months, and I know they were close. Please show me how I can be a blessing, not a burden. Amen."

That meant no afternoon nap for Logan. Instead, he changed both beds—Tabitha had brought two sets of linen—then hung the towels in the bathroom. It wasn't sparkling, but he'd seen worse. He'd find some bleach and clean properly in the morning. For now, he wanted to get this laundry on and ask Mr. Thomas if he could help with dinner, like he'd do if he was staying with family.

After all, he'd been treating this place as his second home since the Thanksgiving of his junior year. Trent had invited Logan home for the holiday after finding he'd never experienced a proper American Thanksgiving. In the years since, he'd often given thanks for being assigned to room with Trent in his freshman year. To say he wasn't close to his family was an understatement, geographically and emotionally. Thanksgiving hadn't just been his first home-cooked American Thanksgiving meal. It had been his first experience of family since he'd started high school.

It had also been the first time he'd met Tabitha. He'd already met Tiffany, Tabitha's identical twin sister, at college when she'd stopped by the dorm to see Trent. Was identical twin the correct term, given they were triplets? Whatever.

Trent had always talked about Tabitha and Tiffany as though they were a single unit—Tabby-and-Tiffy. Perhaps Logan had also been guilty of thinking of the sisters as a single unit, identical in more than just looks. If so, he'd been wrong. Maybe this was his opportunity to get to know Tabitha better.

She preferred Tabby, but he'd been introduced to her as Tabitha, and that was how he thought of her. Tabitha was the name of a woman who was pretty and kind and gracious, a woman known for her good works. Tabby . . . well, Tabby reminded him of a cat. A self-centered, sleepy cat.

And there was nothing sleepy about Tabitha Thomas.

CHAPTER TWO

Logan made his way downstairs, loaded the sheets into the machine, then headed into the kitchen/dining area. Albert Thomas was sitting at the kitchen counter, an assortment of papers in front of him.

"Settled in all right?" Mr. Thomas asked. "Anything you need?"

"Do you have ice?" Logan took a seat at the kitchen counter. "I need to ice and elevate my leg. Too much riding and too little downtime over the last couple of days. And I'm feeling it now."

"No problem." Mr. Thomas gathered his papers into a pile and slid off his seat. "Martha installed one of those fancy plumbed-in refrigerators with chilled water and ice on tap. I guess you want it in a Ziplock bag?"

"Yes, please." Logan rose to head to the fridge. He didn't want to cause more work for Tabby or her father.

"I'll get it," Mr. Thomas said. "You head into the family room and put your feet up."

That sounded perfect. Logan stretched out on the long sofa and rested his bad foot on the footrest. Oh, what a relief after the juddering of the motorcycle and hobbling up and down the inn stairs.

"Here you go." Mr. Thomas handed him a Ziplock bag full of ice and a clean tea towel to wrap it in. He'd obviously dealt with sports injuries before—no surprise, given Trent had played high school football.

"Thank you."

"Didn't Trent tell me you were heading to Europe this spring?"

"Yeah. My first actual holiday in the three years since I graduated." Logan shook his head. "I'd planned to walk the Camino, but munted my ankle going after some newbie who thought they could ski a black diamond. I got off lightly, all things considered. The moon boot is fine for getting around the house, but no good for hiking."

"Glad you're okay. So . . . the Camino?" Mr. Thomas asked.

"The Camino de Santiago—"

"The Way of St. James."

"That's right. It's an ancient pilgrimage to the Church of St. James in Santiago in northern Spain. I was planning to do the Camino Portugues, which starts in Lisbon and is a little over six hundred kilometers—four hundred miles." Plenty of time to reflect on his past, present, and possible future.

"So around four hundred miles more than you're currently able to walk."

"Pretty much." Logan stretched his leg, flexing his good ankle. "The resort physio—physical therapist—gave me a bunch of exercises to do. She also recommended I join a gym and do some weight work, and make sure someone monitored my progress. Any suggestions?"

"There's a full sports center with physical therapists up at the country club. There's also a new person setting up shop on Main Street—I think he's Australian. Otherwise, you'll have to head to Walla Walla."

An Aussie in town sounded a lot more promising than weekly trips to Walla Walla.

Lord, coming to Trinity Lakes was Your idea, so I'm going to trust there is a suitable physio here in town.

"As for the gym, you should check with Tabby. I'm sure some of the teens at the rowing club would know where the local gyms are."

"Thanks. I'll do that. When does she finish work?"

"She usually finishes at around six at this time of year." Mr. Thomas's phone beeped. He checked the notification, then placed the phone back on the kitchen counter. "Earlier in winter, and closer to sunset in the middle of summer."

"What does she do at the rowing club?"

Trent hadn't said she had a job apart from the inn, and Tabitha had never given any indication she was a rower or interested in water sports in general.

"She's the duty manager—greets customers, looks after club members, supervises the teenagers who work after school, takes payments, that kind of thing. She also does some general admin."

"The same kind of thing she does here."

"Yes, although she also does all the cooking and cleaning here. I don't have time, especially at this time of year."

Logan remembered Trent saying how his father, a CPA, worked all hours during tax season.

"I would have thought running the inn would be a full-time job . . . unless you have employees as well?" Surely they had hired help.

"Tabby took over everything when Martha died. I've tried telling her to hire someone, but she refuses."

"I know I haven't seen her for a while, but she looks tired."

"I'm sure she is. I've considered suggesting she give up her job at the rowing club, but it gets her out of the house and gives her the opportunity to spend time with people her own age."

It sounded like Tabitha was doing too much. Like Logan's father. Like his mother. Like too many people he knew.

"Do you have plans for dinner, or would you like to join us?" Mr. Thomas asked. "We eat at around six thirty."

"Thank you. I'll cook if you like." Cooking wasn't his strong point, but he could follow a recipe as well as anyone.

"Tonight is taco salad, so it's under control—the chili is in the slow cooker, and the salad fixings are in the refrigerator."

"I'm happy to help. I don't want to be a burden."

"I'm sure Tabby will appreciate the help. She tends to take on too much."

"I had noticed."

"She needs to learn to say no . . . but that's the only suggestion she'll say no to." He gave a grim laugh.

"It can be hard to say no, even when we already have too much on our plates." Something he'd learned in college.

"This walk . . . you said it's a pilgrimage. A Christian pilgrimage, I assume, if it's named for St. James."

"It started as a Christian pilgrimage, but now people from all walks of life do it, for all sorts of reasons."

"And what were your reasons? Were you planning to walk as a pilgrim, or were you going as a guide?" Mr. Thomas asked. "Don't feel you have to answer if you don't want to."

Logan took a deep breath. He did want to. He wanted to share with someone who might understand in some small way . . . and Albert Thomas might understand in a way Logan's own workaholic father didn't.

Sure, Mr. Thomas might work all hours during tax season, but that was only a season. He'd always taken the summer off to spend with his children. Trent had shared endless stories of their family camping adventures in the years before football took over his free time.

"I'd planned to walk as a pilgrimage, to take some time out to consider what I should be doing with my life."

"That's a noble plan. What prompted the decision? What's changed, that you now feel it's time to figure out what you want in life?"

What had changed?

"It's more that nothing has changed—not for me, at least." Logan paused to collect his thoughts.

Mr. Thomas didn't say anything. That was one more thing Logan had always admired about Mr. Thomas. He didn't feel the need to talk just because no one else was talking. He wasn't afraid of silence.

"I went back to New Zealand for Christmas and got the usual lecture from my father about settling down and focusing on building a career." Which would be a lot easier if he had any idea what kind of career he wanted to build. His degree was social science—something his father said was a waste of time and money—but his background was football, and his work experience was mostly outdoor activities like skiing and surfing.

"From what you've told me in previous visits, there's nothing new in that. So why did it bother you this time?"

"The inevitable questions from my grandmother about when was I going to find a nice girl, settle down, and give her great-grandchildren."

"That sounds like grandmothers everywhere."

"It seemed like all my adult cousins are engaged or married or buying houses or having babies. Even my youngest sister has a boyfriend—and she's only sixteen."

"And how did that feel?" Mr. Thomas was wasted as a tax accountant. He would have made a great counselor. If Logan's dad were more like Mr. Thomas, maybe they'd have a relationship based on mutual respect rather than mutual disapproval. Logan resented his father's workaholic ways, and Dad resented what he perceived as Logan's dead-end degree and directionless existence.

"I guess it made me feel like life—proper life—was passing me by."

"Did it occur to you that the cousin who is married with a baby—or one on the way—was looking at you and hearing your plans for skiing and walking the Camino and working at summer camp in Trinity Lakes and wondering why they're stuck in wherever they are when they could be adventuring around the world, like you are?"

"A couple of them said something along those lines, but I didn't take them seriously. They could do it if they wanted to."

"But could they?" There was a hint of challenge in the question.

"What do you mean?"

"You've had a lot of advantages other people haven't had. You have the right to live and work here in the USA as well as in New Zealand."

And Australia and England, but Logan didn't want to say that.

"You went through college on what must have been a decent scholarship, because you don't appear to have any student loans."

His scholarship had been good but not great, and Dad had covered his dorm fees.

"You got drafted into the NFL, which comes with a solid starting salary. Even if you didn't last long."

His short-lived NFL career had paid off the essentials—his tax bill, his student loans, and his motorcycle. It had also left him with a gaping hole—what was he supposed to do with his life? So he'd fallen back to what he knew best—sports. And young people.

"All that gave you choices other people haven't had, and you've taken advantage of those choices."

"I hear a 'but' in there."

Mr. Thomas smiled. "But now you're feeling some disquiet

in your spirit. That could be God telling you it's time to reconsider your choices or make a new choice. Tell me, what gave you the idea to walk the Camino?"

"It kind of came out of nowhere. I was sitting next to this guy on my last flight to New Zealand and we got talking about what we did. He'd spent the summer as a Camino guide and told me all about it."

"And?"

"I did some research and felt led to put aside time to do the walk. It's a spiritual pilgrimage, a disconnection from my normal routine—"

Mr. Thomas laughed. "Normal routine? Your routine is anything but normal."

"Fair point." He had a routine—ski instructor, summer camp counselor, tour guide, surf instructor—but it was a long way from what most people considered normal. "Anyway, I liked the idea of hiking through Spain and Portugal, so I looked into it. I realized most people do the trip solo, so that's what I decided to do."

"You decided." Mr. Thomas's tone was the short matter-of-fact tone people like counselors—or tax advisers—used when they were about to drop a truth bomb.

"Yeah . . ."

"You, a Christian, decided to walk the Camino as a spiritual pilgrimage, but you didn't talk that through with God?"

Ouch. "I guess I did the Gideon's fleece thing. Asked Him to make it obvious if there was something I should be doing instead."

"And now you're here, in Trinity Lakes, with an injury that's not serious and will heal, but which has put a stop to your plans to walk the Camino."

Not serious? It hadn't been serious the first time he'd twisted his ankle, back in high school. Or the second, in college. Or the third, in his first and only NFL pre-season. Each injury had taken longer and longer to heal, and the last had ended his fledgling football career. His ankle would heal, but would it heal in time for him to start at summer camp as scheduled? He had no idea.

"That sounds a lot like a fleece to me." Mr. Thomas sat back in his chair and crossed his wrists over his stomach. "I wonder if you were planning to walk the Camino as an excuse, a spiritualized evasion of where God wants you to be."

There it was—the truth bomb.

"He is God. He can talk to us any place, any time. The only proviso is that we have to be prepared to listen."

And another truth bomb. Mr. Thomas was firing on all cylinders today.

God, Mr. Thomas is right. I didn't ask You when I should have, but I'm asking now. Please show me where You want me. Use this time to give me some direction for the future. And please help Tabitha. She needs You even more than I do.

DESPITE HER UNEXPECTED GUEST, Tabby had made it to work only seven minutes behind her scheduled start time. Fortunately, Hannah was a laid-back boss and a good friend, and her job at the rowing club similar to her role at the B&B, but with more customer interaction. The B&B tended to attract couples —young couples, middle-aged couples, older couples. No families, no children, no teenagers. The rowing club's customers ranged from teenagers to seniors, with plenty of college students and families during the summer season.

The afternoon passed quickly. Tabby was exhausted by the time she got back to the inn at the thought of her never-ending to-do list.

Not least, getting started on clearing out Gran's suite so they could get her bedroom and bathroom renovated and redecorated and make the room available for guests. After that, they'd need to repeat the process in Gran's living room and kitchen, so they could make the whole suite available. Then—

No.

Stop.

She had to focus on one thing at once or she'd get overwhelmed. Well, even more overwhelmed.

She was always working, always moving, always doing. Even though she'd prepped dinner before leaving for work, she would still have to clean up afterward, then finish the laundry before bed, prep breakfast for the guests, and set the table. And somehow find the time and energy to read the novel Hannah had chosen for book club.

Maybe she'd cancel this month. It was tempting, except it was her one chance to get away from work for a couple of hours and spend time with her friends. Sometimes they even discussed the book.

First, she needed to put the dirty sheets from Trent's room on to wash. If she did that now, she could get them in the dryer after dinner, which would mean she wouldn't be behind tomorrow.

She headed to the laundry, but there were no sheets in the hamper. No sheets in the washing machine either, dirty or clean. So where were they? They must still be in his room. Bother.

Okay. She'd fold the load of towels she'd shoved into the dryer just before Logan arrived. She opened the dryer to find navy sheets—Trent's sheets—not the white guest towels she'd expected. Not only had Logan changed both beds, but he'd also washed the sheets and loaded them into the dryer. So where were the towels? In the laundry basket? No. She surveyed the room. There they were, on the shelf, folded as perfectly as if she or Gran had folded them.

That was unexpected but welcome. She stacked the clean

towels and linens onto her cleaning trolley, then headed to the kitchen to finish prepping dinner.

She walked into the kitchen to find Dad stirring the chili she'd left in the slow cooker while Logan chopped tomatoes. In front of him were bowls of shredded lettuce, grated cheese, and homemade guacamole. Dad looked up as she walked in.

"Perfect timing. Everything is ready. Grab yourself a drink and sit down." The kitchen counter was already set for dinner. Another pleasant surprise that was no doubt Logan's doing. It wasn't that Dad didn't help—he did when he could. But tax season was silly season, so the best he could do was watch the front desk weekday afternoons while she worked at the rowing club.

"Logan, thank you for folding the towels and washing the sheets. That's a huge help."

"No problem. It's the least I could do."

"He's set the dining room table for breakfast as well," Dad said as he set the bowl of chili on the table.

"This all looks great," Tabby said.

"You did all the hard work." Logan set the salads and salsa in the center of the counter. "We just pulled it all together."

Just. His unsolicited help here and in the laundry had saved her a couple of hours of work. A man who did housework without being asked? She hadn't known such a man existed. So much for getting over her crush.

———

AFTER DINNER, Tabby stood to clear the table.

"I'll clear." Logan pushed his chair back and gathered their plates.

With Logan helping, clearing the table, and cleaning the kitchen was finished in half the time it usually took her. Dad disappeared into his study—he'd get another two or three hours of work done before bed tonight.

What would she do? Thanks to Logan, she was actually caught up on all her tasks for today. She'd even managed to box up a generous serving of leftover taco salad to take to work tomorrow. She'd reheat the meat-and-bean mixture at work and leave it on a picnic table outside the rowing club for the Junk Man, along with a thermos of black coffee.

The Junk Man was a local almost-hobo who worked for the city, keeping the parks and other public land tidy and free of trash, caring for injured wildlife, and occasionally rescuing small children. He appeared near the rowing club at the same time every afternoon. He'd eat and drink whatever she'd prepared, leaving the empty container and thermos on the veranda when he finished.

"You've been working all day. You need to sit down and relax. How would you like to sit outside and watch the sunset?" Logan asked.

She should say no because she should take this extra hour to get started on clearing out Gran's suite or retire to her room to read the novel Hannah had chosen for book club. But clearing Gran's suite was a daytime task—she didn't want to disturb the paying guests in the room next to Gran's—and she was too tired to pay attention to a novel.

She should say no because sitting and watching the sunset with a handsome man had the potential to be romantic, and she didn't want to give anyone the wrong idea—herself, Logan, or the local gossips who could be relied on to misinterpret at least half of any story.

She should say no because this was Logan, her long-time secret crush, and there was no way she could relax in his presence. No way she'd want to relax, to let her guard down. Logan, the man her brother had warned her against the first time they'd met. Wild Logan Wylde.

Maybe this was her chance to offer a Christian witness, to show him that people didn't have to attend wild parties to have fun.

"I'd love to watch the sunset."

Would spending time with Logan without Trent directing the conversation help her get over her crush? Or would getting to know Logan make it worse? There was only one way to find out.

"Would you like something to drink?" she asked. "Coffee? Hot chocolate? Iced tea? Soda?"

"Diet soda, if you have one. I'll get it."

"Sure—they'll be in the guest refrigerator. That's the one on the left." She gestured toward the two huge refrigerators beside the pantry.

Logan opened the door and grabbed a can. "What can I get you?" he asked.

"I have decaf iced tea over here, thanks."

Once they had their drinks, Tabby led the way onto the front balcony outside the guest lounge where they sat on two perfectly positioned Adirondack chairs. Tabby would have preferred the rear veranda, overlooking the fields behind the house. The view wasn't as pretty as the view over the lake, but it was more private. The lakefront was a popular path to promenade in the evenings. If any of the local gossips saw Tabby and Logan together on the front veranda, they'd have them engaged by morning.

"What do you plan to do while you're here?" Tabby asked.

"Get over this ankle injury. I need to start by seeing a physical therapist. Anyone you'd recommend?"

"Your best option is the country club," Tabby said.

"Your dad mentioned the country club. I assumed it was just a golf course and a fancy restaurant."

"It's more than that. Wayne Gilbertson made a fortune playing pro golf, and he's plowed that money back into the town—the rowing club, the golf club, the country club. The country club has a full gym, and a physical therapy team which specializes in sports injuries."

"Are there any other options? Your father suggested Adam someone. Do you know him?"

"Adam Lancaster is new to town—he's married to Leah's best friend, Melanie. He's set up practice in the front room of their house."

"Leah?"

"Leah runs the organic food shop in town." Of course. Logan wasn't a local, so he wouldn't know Tabby's friends.

"Then I'll have to check Leah's place out as well."

"You eat organic?" Tabby asked. "The inn isn't organic . . ." Was that going to be a problem? She wanted her guests to be comfortable, even her uninvited, unexpected guests.

"I eat healthy. Organic shops generally have a better selection of healthy food."

"So no burgers?"

"I love a good burger—which means a burger made with meat, not fat and fillers."

Not a surprise. All the Australians in town were into red meat and lots of it, so she didn't expect anything different from a Kiwi. "Then you should definitely check out Leah's store."

"Where is it?"

"Near the Emporium. It's a small town. You'll find it. Anything else?"

"Find a gym. Somewhere other than the country club."

Tabby had never needed to join a gym, as her jobs kept her active enough. The only gym she knew of was the one at the country club. It did offer tourist memberships . . . at tourist prices. Probably well out of Logan's budget. "What kind of gym?"

"Something relatively low-key, with a good set of basic machines and some free weights. Your dad said you might know the best place. Or someone at the rowing club might know."

"I'll ask tomorrow. Or you could ask Adam." She took a sip of her tea.

"I'll get in touch with him tomorrow. For now, let's enjoy the sunset." He gestured out over the lake.

Tabby turned to look at the view. "I've always enjoyed watching the sun go down over the lake."

"Or watching the sun rise over the mountains. I bet that's beautiful."

"It is, but mornings always tend to be busy here." Cooking breakfast for her guests, cleaning the kitchen and the guest lounge while she waited for them to check out or leave for the day, making up or freshening the guest rooms, and grabbing a quick lunch before heading off to work at the rowing club.

"No time to sit and watch the sun wake up?"

"Unfortunately, no. Gran and I would often sit out here with a cup of chamomile tea on a summer evening." She missed their long talks as the sun went down, discussing their respective days and the people they'd met. Gran always liked to finish with a prayer of thanksgiving for the gifts God had given them and the people He'd brought their way.

She'd missed this—sitting, resting, talking. Praying. Getting to know someone. She didn't have the time—or energy—to chat with her guests most days, let alone talk with God.

"I can see why. It's almost perfect. You know what would make it better?" he asked.

"Better?" That was an easy question. "A swinging chair. I'd love to be able to sit out here and swing. One that's big enough for two or three people, so I could sit on it with my feet up and read a book." In an alternate world, a fantasy world, a world where she had time to put her feet up and read.

Logan laughed. "That's a great idea, but it wasn't what I was thinking. I was more thinking of the view." He gestured to the lakeshore and park in front of them. "What's with that?" He pointed. "The boat shed."

"It's been abandoned as long as I can remember. The Gilbertson's family trust owns the land from the boat shed to the rowing club." Tabby gestured away to the right, toward the rowing club. "But no one knows who owns the boat shed, and no one has done any maintenance in years."

Perhaps decades. Certainly not in her memory. The building was over thirty feet wide and almost twice as long, giving enough space to store at least half a dozen rowboats and sailing dinghies and their associated paraphernalia. Gran had stories of sailing around the lake as a child, back when the boat shed was a thriving holiday business.

But now the lack of maintenance showed in the row of grimy windows and peeling paint.

"Why is it still there?" Logan asked. "It looks like a health hazard."

"No one knows who owns it, so no one can do anything about it."

"I thought small towns were hotbeds of gossip where everyone knew everything about everyone else's business." Logan chuckled.

"That's not far from the truth, but the town gossips have drawn a blank on the boat shed. Gran always said the Rhondas knew more than all the doctors, ministers, and lawyers in town combined, but even the Rhondas don't know who owns the boat shed."

"The Rhondas?"

"Rhonda Ingalls and Rhonda Turner, the two main town gossips. Rhonda Ingalls's son is a local realtor, so she always knows who's moving in, out, and around. Rhonda Turner is a widow who has dedicated herself to good works." Which meant knowing everything about everyone. Neither of the Rhondas were malicious, but if the Rhondas knew something, it wasn't going to stay private.

"Looks like the kind of place small boys would want to use as a secret hideout and bigger boys would use for vaping and smoking and drinking and whatever the rebels of Trinity Lakes like to get up to on Saturday night when their parents and pastors aren't watching."

Yes, small boys had once used the boat shed as a secret hideout. So had small girls.

"Have you ever been inside?" Logan asked.

"A few times. But not since we were kids." Her tone was light, dismissive, as though there was nothing worth mentioning.

"What's it like?"

"A mess. Dangerous. The floorboards have rotted in places, so it's not safe. And there's birds and rats and other pests." The Junk Man was the only person who'd been near the place in years. "It's locked now. No one can get inside."

"Sounds like there's a story there."

There was. But knowing the story and being willing to share the story were not the same thing. No one knew except Tabby, Tiffy, Trent, and the Junk Man. And he'd sworn their same seven-year-old pinkie promise to never tell.

CHAPTER THREE

Logan arrived at the physical therapist's office at ten o'clock the next morning. As Tabitha had said, it was the front room of a regular house, a house that had been renovated to include a work-from-home practice.

The physio, Adam Lancaster, spent a little time talking through Logan's medical history, then examined his ankle. He struck Logan as a nice guy and a competent physio. If the artwork on the walls was any indication, he was also a Christian—something Tabby hadn't mentioned.

And Adam was Australian, which wasn't Kiwi but was close enough that they had the instant rapport of outsiders in a foreign land as they compared notes on places they'd been and people they'd met.

"So how'd you end up here?" Logan asked as Adam poked and prodded his ankle.

"I developed a range of protein powders—Blitz Mix. Melanie found me on Instagram and convinced Leah to stock my products," Adam said. "I took Melanie out to dinner to say thank you, we got married last year, and here we are." The look on

Adam's face said there was more to the story than his short summary.

"I've bought Blitz Mix powders before. Great flavors."

"Thanks. I try. What about you?" Adam asked. "What brings you to Trinity Lakes?"

"I'll be a counselor at Trinity Lakes Summer Camp, and I'd planned to spend a couple of months hiking in Portugal and Spain before that."

"Any particular reason?"

"I'd planned to hike the Camino de Santiago." Logan stretched his leg and picked up the moon boot.

"I've heard of it, although I haven't done it myself." Adam stepped back, sat behind his computer, and clicked on the keys.

"There's a whole bunch of different routes starting as far away as Rome or further. I was planning on doing the Camino Portugues, which starts in Portugal."

"That's not as far as Rome, but it's still a long way in a moon boot." Adam's half-smile showed he had the typical Aussie sense of humor. "That tells me why you're not in Spain but doesn't tell me how you ended up here."

"I was roommates with Trent Thomas in college, and he suggested I come and stay at his place."

"Trent Thomas? The name doesn't sound familiar." Adam clicked on the computer mouse, and the printer whirred.

"His family owns the Lakeview Inn, the B&B on Main Street overlooking the lake."

"I know the place." Adam offered Logan half a dozen sheets of printed paper. "Here are some exercises I recommend you do once or twice daily. We don't want you dependent on the moon boot—the more gentle exercise you can do, the quicker you'll get out of it."

Logan took the papers and glanced at them.

"Any questions?" Adam asked.

"They all look fairly self-explanatory." This wasn't Logan's first ankle injury. "Now I'm looking for a gym and a church." He gestured toward the picture of what looked like Jesus raising the widow's son from the dead. "Where do you go? I assume you go somewhere."

"Melanie and I go to Trinity Life Church. I've also been to Trinity Lakes Community Church and enjoyed it."

Trinity Lakes Community Church sounded familiar. Perhaps that was where the Thomas family went.

"I'll check those out. Any gym recommendations?"

"There's an excellent gym at the country club—"

"Not my scene." His experience of country clubs was limited, but teenage movies and the stories from his college friends painted a picture of serious posers, not serious athletes. Not that he was a serious athlete anymore. Which was why he'd come to Adam, rather than one of the specialist sports physios at the country club.

"Then your best bet is the YMCA. It doesn't have all the expensive equipment and fancy classes they have at the country club, but it's a solid gym with all the basic equipment. Check it out."

"I will. Thanks."

"Just no overdoing it. Rest is the best cure for injuries like yours, especially in the first few weeks."

Weeks?

"Yes, I mean weeks. Not days."

Logan's worry must have shown in his face. As long as he was healed before camp began—it was bad enough that he was missing the Camino. He didn't want to let the camp down. Or the campers. From what he'd been told, Camp Trinity had a different group of campers each week, to give as many children and teens as possible the summer camp experience.

"I'd like to see you once a week. In the meantime, here are some daily exercises you can do." Adam pointed to the sheets he'd printed off. "It's going to take six to eight weeks—

minimum—to heal. You said it's not your first ankle injury, but let's try and make sure it's your last."

Logan would listen. He'd relax, RICE, and roll his ankle through the prescribed range-of-motion exercises. Whatever it took to heal and get on with figuring out what he was going to do for the rest of his life.

———

TABBY ARRIVED at work ten minutes early with a spring in her step. She placed her purse in the drawer below the reception desk and powered up the computer as Hannah emerged from the changing rooms.

"Becky said a cute Australian on a very loud, very expensive motorcycle bought a coffee from her yesterday, then headed to the inn." Hannah picked up a pen from the desk.

"Logan's from New Zealand." Tabby corrected Hannah without thinking.

That was a mistake.

Hannah tap-tap-tapped her pen on the counter. "New Zealand. Like the hobbits. Was it Logan from New Zealand I saw sitting on your front veranda when I drove past at quarter to dawn this morning?"

"What? Who?"

"I haven't seen him since you invited me for Thanksgiving dinner—what was it? Four years ago?"

"Four? I think it was your senior year at college. You came home for Thanksgiving, but your mother had taken your sisters to Florida." Tabby had no particular interest in Susannah Gilbertson—she much preferred Hannah's Granny Gracie—and she had zero interest in talking about Logan.

"That sounds right. My dear mother 'forgot' to tell me the must-attend family Thanksgiving was in Florida because Dan couldn't possibly travel to Trinity. Then it was my fault for not knowing, therefore ruining family Thanksgiving." Hannah had long-standing issues with her self-absorbed mother. "Anyway, we're not talking about my family. We're talking about Logan. He really is a fine specimen of masculinity."

"Yes, Logan is staying, so it must have been him you saw. None of my paying guests would be up that early." Tabby turned and gave her own version of Tom Selleck's raised eyebrows. "Anyway, why were you noticing? I thought you had a boyfriend."

"Why is Logan in Trinity Lakes?"

"He's got a job as a counselor at the summer camp and needs somewhere to stay until training starts."

"Camp doesn't start until May, so why is Logan in Trinity Lakes two months early?" Hannah could be like a dog with a bone once she got an idea in her head.

"He was snowboarding in Canada with Trent, had an accident, and twisted his ankle. He'd been planning to do some big walk in Europe and couldn't. So Trent 'invited' him to stay at the inn." Tabby raised her fingers in air quotes.

"How do you feel about having an uninvited guest?"

"He's helping around the place, which I'm thankful for." And she'd write that in her gratitude journal if she ever found the time.

"What does Logan from New Zealand do when he's not hanging around Trinity Lakes, waiting for summer camp to start?"

"Short-term tourism-type jobs. He moves around a lot." All she knew was what she'd read on the postcards he'd sent . . . postcards which weren't even addressed to her.

"Hmm." Tap-tap-tap. "So he spent who knows how much on a college education and now works short-term low-wage jobs yet rides an expensive motorcycle. Interesting." Her words were bland, not indicating a question or a judgment.

"You tell me."

"He did graduate college, right? What was his major?"

"Something to do with sports, I think." Tabby realized she didn't actually know. "He was on the football team with Trent. Special teams. I'm sure Trent told me Logan got drafted to the NFL, but that can't be right." Logan was a wanderer and an adventurer.

"Football would explain his buff physique. He looks like a sportsman." Hannah would know, as she came from a family of pro sportspeople.

"If you could check out his physique while driving past the inn, you were paying too much attention to the scenery and not enough attention to the road." Tabby shook her head in mock disapproval. "I wouldn't want the good sheriff to hear about that."

"Never mind Sheriff Thompson. He's got enough to worry about with Leah and the man she's not dating. I want to hear all about Logan."

"There's nothing to tell," Tabby said. Nothing except that Logan reminded her of all the best qualities of Heath Ledger in *Ten Things I Hate About You*—blond corkscrew curls that begged to be touched and tugged, to see if they'd straighten out or spring back. A smile that could brighten even the worst of winter weather. A countenance—to borrow from Jane Austen and high school English—that was always open and friendly. Whenever he spoke to someone, he always gave them his full attention, asked insightful questions, and acted as though he wanted to know the answer, as though nothing in the world was more important than their conversation.

At first, Tabby had thought he was interested in her. Then she'd seen him talking to old Mrs. Ingalls with the same rapt attention—Rhonda Ingalls was lovely but always had a lot to say—and with Kyla Ferguson, who was a lot less lovely and also had a lot to say.

Anyway, teenage Tabby had soon realized Logan wasn't

interested in her in a romantic way—for which she was both grateful and resentful. It had been a blow to her ego for about five minutes, until she reminded herself he wasn't a Christian, and he wasn't going to stay.

But she still had half a crush on Logan. She remembered the first time they met as though it were yesterday. She'd sat opposite him at Thanksgiving dinner, and he'd literally taken her breath away with the combination of his good looks and adorable accent. Breathless, unfortunately, did not make a good first impression. She'd barely been able to get a word out, even when he asked her the most basic questions.

His looks had matured over the years, and she'd managed to overcome her initial tongue-tied behavior. Now they were somewhere between acquaintances and friends, and he'd come to Trinity Lakes every Thanksgiving since that first year, as well as a couple of Christmases when he'd been unable to spend the holiday with his family in New Zealand.

He joked that the Thomases were his second family, which made it easier for Tabby to ignore her initial attraction and treat him like a second brother. Opposites attract, as the cliché said, and they were opposites in everything. He'd traversed the globe with no ties to anywhere or anyone. She'd barely left Trinity Lakes, never traveled, because she was needed here. He was the extrovert, the life of the party. She was the introvert who invariably organized the party. He'd dated innumerable blonde bombshells, including her own sister. She'd dated exactly one guy, who'd left and gone to college. Logan had never held a steady job. She'd been working for the family business since before she'd been legally old enough to draw a paycheck.

They could have overcome those differences. The one difference they couldn't overcome was faith.

She was a Christian.

He was not.

CHAPTER FOUR

Monday morning dawned damp, with clouds in the sky and a fine mist over the lake. Tabby didn't need the weather forecast to tell her rain was coming. Hopefully it would hold off long enough for her guests to check out. The Lakeview Inn was a grand old lady—elegant and proud but missing some of the niceties of modern living, like a garage or covered carport. She'd already had more than one online review from a guest complaining they'd gotten wet dragging their oversized cases a whole twenty feet from the shelter of the veranda to their car. She didn't need more Negative Nellies ruining her ratings.

Rain.

Maybe she could start cleaning out Gran's suite. She'd been putting off the task for too long already. She should get in there, if for no other reason than that Dad needed to know he had all the tax invoices, receipts, and sundry paperwork he'd need to finish the inn's taxes for last year.

Only the task wasn't one she wanted to do alone . . . or was that what she'd been telling herself as a way of delaying the inevitable?

"Penny for them." Logan ambled into the kitchen, favoring his good leg. He perched on one of the bar stools facing the kitchen island.

"Trying to decide what to do today." Her phone beeped with a notification, and she picked it up. Hannah. She expected it to be a quiet day today, so Tabby didn't need to come in until two.

"Looks like rain," Logan said.

"I'm hoping it holds off until checkout so the guests can make a dry getaway." Tabby got a tray of eggs out of the fridge and cracked them into a large bowl one by one. Today was omelet day, and she was going to prepare an additional over-sized frittata and salad for one of the young mothers at church. Rhonda Turner had quietly mentioned that Ruthie Johnson was having trouble adjusting to motherhood after a difficult birth. A meal might help.

"Any plans for today?" Logan asked.

"That text was from Hannah," Tabby said. "I don't have to work until two this afternoon. Is there anything you'd like me to take you to or show you?"

"Not with my munted ankle, thanks. And I'm sure you have better things to do than babysit an uninvited freeloader."

"But not unwelcome." Tabby was surprised to realize that was the truth. Despite her earlier misgivings, she'd enjoyed having Logan around these last few days. He'd definitely been more of a help than a hinderance.

"Is there anything I can give you a hand with?" Logan asked. "I can't sit around doing nothing while you're working."

Tabby cracked another three eggs before responding. It was one thing to allow Logan to set the table or fold towels—not that she'd asked him to do either. He'd noticed what needed doing and completed the chores. He'd even mowed the lawns on their ride-on mower.

It was another to ask for his help in clearing out Gran's

room. But it wasn't a task she wanted to tackle alone. Logan could help. But Logan wasn't family. He was a guest.

"You look like you have an idea, but you don't want to ask," Logan said. "Spit it out."

"We . . . I . . . need to clear out Gran's room. It's sitting vacant, and Gran would have hated that."

"Are you going to clear out Martha's room?" Dad came into the kitchen and opened the fridge to get the milk and juice for the breakfast bar. "It's time. The fifteenth of April will be here before we know it . . ."

"And it wouldn't do for the town's tax adviser to be late in filing his own taxes. I know."

"Besides, Martha wouldn't want her rooms sitting unused like some kind of shrine," Dad said. "She'd want us to get the rooms renovated in time to catch at least some of the summer visitors."

"Is that even possible?" It was less than five weeks until Anzac Day and the town's annual commemorative football game. While summer didn't officially start until Memorial Day, the inn was usually booked out over Anzac weekend—the last weekend in April—and grew steadily busier . . . which meant more work for Tabby to cram into her already-busy days.

"We won't know until we start," Dad said. "I expect we'll need to renovate the bathroom, but I'm hoping the bedroom will only need a spruce up. Jasper Cohen does quality work, and he'll quote a fair price. That will give us one more room for guests. Make the house earn a few more dollars."

Dad was right. If she didn't get started now, she'd be in the full summer rush and September would be here before she'd even cracked the door open.

Gran had always been pragmatic when it came to money. Probably the result of having been raised in a house that was falling down around her with no way to pay for repairs. But that had changed, and they'd managed to renovate most of the property over the last few years—everything except the family bedrooms and Gran's suite—even while supporting Tiffany and Trent through college.

"What about the kitchenette and living room?" Dad asked. "Would you prefer to keep it as a suite, or replace the kitchen with a bathroom and turn it into another guest room? Or a family bedroom. Then you and Tiffy wouldn't have to share."

"Tiffy is hardly here anyway. She doesn't need a room of her own." That much Tabby did know. But Dad's other questions? She had no idea. Renovating would mean too many decisions she didn't have the time or headspace to consider.

"First things first," Dad said. "Get started."

"I can help," Logan said.

"Are you sure?" She didn't want to take advantage of him.

"I don't have anything else to do. Besides, it will be easier with two of us working."

"Thank you. I couldn't face doing it alone." Tabby tipped a robust mix of chopped ham and mushrooms, grated cheese, and egg into four frying pans, then adjusted the heat to let them cook. She turned back to the men and gripped the counter. "It's too much. Too many memories."

"I know, honey." Dad gave her hand a squeeze.

"I'm not much good with moving or carrying stuff right now, but I can sort and clean," Logan said.

"You serve breakfast. I'll manage the cleanup and deal with checkout," Dad said. "You two head up there as soon as you're ready."

"Thank you." Tabby's eyes misted. The words seemed insignificant in comparison to the metaphorical weight that lifted from her shoulders.

———

"Have you ever been in here before?" Tabby asked as they climbed the stairs together half an hour later.

"No. Your grandmother was usually in the kitchen when I stayed."

"The kitchen was where she felt most at home." Tabby still half-expected Gran to pop out from the pantry every time she went into the kitchen.

"I could tell." Logan's words were as calming as his presence. "Have you been in here since . . ."

"Since she died?" Tabby asked. "Only once, to get the clothes she wanted to be buried in. And Dad came in once to find the finance stuff."

She turned the doorknob and opened the door slowly, as if she was trying not to disturb whoever was in the room. Or whatever. The mere act of opening the door roused dozens of dust bunnies. Tabby sneezed into her elbow.

She opened the door wider and ushered Logan in. As he looked around, curious, she took in the familiar space, seeing evidence of Gran on every shelf, in every corner, in every piece of furniture.

"The house has an unusual design." Logan turned on his one good heel. "It's like two houses in one. Well, two houses and this guest suite."

"The ancestor who built it had twin daughters who didn't want to be separated, even after they got married. He built it like this so the daughters could still live together, while giving their husbands their own space." Or so Gran had always told her.

Gran's lounge was dark and had the musty smell of a room that had been closed for too long. Tabby crossed the room, pulled back the curtains, and opened the window to let in the fresh spring air. Dust sparkled in the sunlight, lightening and brightening the room.

"It looks like your grandmother," Logan turned on his heels, taking in the room. "Navy and burgundy, florals and paisleys. Good solid furniture. Classic designs, designs that last. And memories."

"Lots of memories. As you can see, this was her living room. There's a small kitchen through that door." Tabby indicated a door at the side of the room next to the main door, on the opposite side from the windows. "Her bedroom is through there, along with an en suite."

"A true granny flat," Logan said.

"A what?" Had Tabby heard him properly?

"Granny flat—a self-contained apartment that's part of a bigger house—somewhere an older teenager or elderly parent or grandparent could live so they're independent, but still close by."

"Makes sense. Yes, a granny flat." Gran would have liked that play on words.

Tabby crossed the room and opened the door into the bedroom. The air had the old-clothes smell of a secondhand store. Logan followed.

"Nice," he said. "A bit dated in comparison with the guest rooms in the west wing, but that's mostly cosmetic. The bedroom furniture looks to be in good nick. You could probably keep it. What's it made from?"

"Probably oak." Tabby ran her fingers along a dusty bookshelf. "It looks original, and the inn's original furniture was all made from the same oak as the floorboards and walls."

"So I'd keep that and focus on updating the decor—repaint or repaper the walls and change the curtains and carpet. Would you use the same color scheme as in the other guest rooms?"

Gran had loved florals, so the wallpaper, curtains, and bedspread were currently three different floral patterns, none of which matched each other, let alone the antique-meets-minimalist aesthetic of the rest of the inn. Random picture frames displayed Bible verses and inspirational quotes—Jeremiah, Proverbs, John, Augustine.

"I . . ." She couldn't stop the tears from welling. The room was uncoordinated to the point of being ugly, but the thought of redecorating felt like losing Gran all over again.

"Hey, you don't have to decide now." Logan put his arm around her shoulder and gave her a brotherly side hug. The gesture was comforting and reassuring. "Where do you want to start?"

"I don't know." Tabby held back a sob, and Logan tugged her a little closer. The hug was . . . nice. Perhaps too nice. She wiped her eyes with her sleeve and edged away from his hold.

"The hardest part about moving is always deciding what to keep and what to throw away," Logan said. "It gets emotional, going through someone's personal possessions. How about we start in the kitchen? It's probably easiest."

"That makes sense." Tabby opened the door. The room was clean and tidy, but the decor was dark and dated. It needed a complete overhaul.

"It's like stepping back in time," Logan said. "I can't remember when I last saw avocado-green Formica. And look at that oven—it's a retro classic." The oversized wall oven was so old, the brown faux-wood vinyl was wearing off the front.

"Gran and Grandpa turned these two bedrooms into an apartment sometime in the eighties, when Grandpa's mother came to live here." Mom, Gran, Grandpa, and Great-grandma. Three generations in one house, just like she'd been raised.

"It looks like it hasn't been renovated since." Logan opened the oven door and peered inside.

"Well, it's not hard to decide what needs to happen in here," Tabby said. "It all needs to come out, no matter whether we decide to keep this as a kitchen or turn it into a bathroom. That doorway is too narrow, and I doubt the plumbing meets code."

"So let's empty the cupboards and see if there's anything

worth keeping," Logan said. "You and your family can figure out what you're going to use the room for another day."

His practical focus made it easy to agree.

Tabby opened the cupboard under the sink to reveal an array of threadbare tea towels, decaying kitchen sponges, a few half-full bottles of cleaning products, and a box of medicines so old she couldn't even read the use-by dates. Who kept their medicines in the kitchen rather than the bathroom?

"This is all trash." Tabby pulled a couple of bottles out of the cupboard. "I should have thought to bring some bags. This lot isn't going to fit in Gran's dinky trash can."

"I grabbed some bags from the main kitchen." Logan pulled a roll of black garbage bags from the pocket of his oversized hoodie. "I think we empty the cupboards, trash the rubbish right away, then come back to anything we're not sure about."

"Sounds like a plan." Tabby was grateful for his presence, his practicality, and his compassion. The combination turned what had seemed impossible into something that felt achievable—they'd finish the kitchen before she had to go to work this afternoon. Maybe tomorrow she'd be able to tackle the desk.

CHAPTER FIVE

None of the guests were checking out today, which meant Tabby didn't need to do a full clean in any of the rooms. She just needed to wait for the guests to leave for the day so she could do a basic service—make the beds, clean the bathroom, and change the towels. That wouldn't take long, so she had some extra time before she needed to leave for the rowing club.

She and Logan had fallen into a routine in the week since he had arrived. Goodness, had it only been a week? He'd slipped into the household routine so well that it felt like longer. Like he'd always lived here. But not like he was part of the family. The more time she spent with him, the more she liked him and the more she had to remind herself that he was all wrong for her.

They'd share a coffee while Tabby prepared breakfast for the guests. When the guests came down to breakfast, Logan would sit on the veranda and work through a series of exercises the PT had given him. Then he'd clear the kitchen while she checked out the guests. One morning, she'd even had time to crack open her Bible and pray.

Then they'd work together to prepare the rooms for the next

visitors. Once they finished, they'd spend an hour or two in Gran's rooms before lunch, and Tabby would head off to work. Logan would get back to the inn in time to check in any new guests, which gave Dad the opportunity to spend another couple of hours in the office.

Now she'd made a start on Gran's room, she wanted to get back up there and keep going, even though Logan wasn't around to help—he'd made his apologies during breakfast, saying he had an appointment with his physical therapist. It didn't take long to clear up from breakfast, load the dishwasher, and clean the kitchen counters. She would usually set the table for tomorrow's breakfast, but she wanted to get back into Gran's suite.

She opened the door to the suite and grabbed one of the archive boxes Dad had given her. The desk had four drawers and a drop-down working surface that rested on two pull-out supports.

Tabitha opened the top drawer. It was overflowing with receipts and bank statements. She picked up a handful and looked at the dates. They all looked to be at least ten years old, if not older. No wonder Dad had taken over managing the B&B finances, because Gran's recordkeeping left a lot to be desired. She'd been in the habit of keeping random receipts in a disorganized shoebox. Tabby then had the unenviable task of sorting through the detritus and organizing the invoices and receipts so her father could produce a set of accounts the IRS would accept.

Tabitha pulled out the desk supports to the side of the top drawer, opened the desk, and rested the lid on the supports. The storage area was surprisingly tidy. There were small drawers inside the lid, where Grandma held useful things like stamps and sticky notes. In the middle were small slots for filing. Tabitha pulled the envelopes out of one. Birthday cards. The next one held Christmas cards, and the others had stationery and empty envelopes. Grandma had been a lot better at looking after pretty stationery than old receipts.

Tabby closed the desk and opened the second drawer, where she found too many pens and pencils to count, in all colors of the rainbow and some colors that definitely weren't seen in nature. Knowing Gran, at least half of them wouldn't work. Gran had an almost pathological fear of throwing away anything that could possibly be used again, even the tiniest pencil stub.

Tabby closed the drawer. She'd sort the pens later.

She opened the long bottom drawer, Gran's wrapping paper drawer. For as long as Tabby could remember, the bottom drawer had always contained neatly folded used wrapping paper—Christmas paper, birthday paper, plain brown paper. She closed the drawer. Not even Tiffy would want recycled wrapping paper. Maybe she could take it to church. It might make a fun activity for the children's ministry. They could have the pens as well. She emptied all the paper and the pens into an archive box, closed the box, and labeled it, "Children's Church."

The next drawer up was full of photo albums. While she desperately wanted to sit down and look through each photo and handwritten caption—to vicariously visit all the cities and countries Gran and Grandad had visited over the years, to mentally plan where she wanted to go and what she wanted to see—there wasn't time today. The albums would have to wait. For now, she wanted to make sure there was nothing else in the drawers, no stray invoices or receipts or anything else Uncle Sam and his minions might find interesting.

One by one, she emptied the albums out of the drawer.

Wait.

What was that?

There, lying between two ancient albums, was an envelope, yellowed with age. She pulled it out and carefully opened the flap. Inside was a single sheet of paper and two photographs.

She emptied the envelope and looked at the photos first. Both were sepia rather than black-and-white monochrome, and both had the crinkled edges of an old studio picture. Very old. One showed a young woman in a long white dress, holding a bouquet, and standing on a veranda overlooking the lake. Was that the old boat shed? Had it once had a veranda? The woman stood next to a bearded man in a suit, holding his arm. The photo looked too old to be Gran and Grandad. Gran's parents, perhaps? Was this one of their wedding photos? Perhaps their only wedding photo.

The other photo was of a sturdy rowing boat pulled up on the lakeshore next to what looked like a brand-new boat shed. Their boat shed? The view was the same as from the inn's front veranda. Interesting.

She put the photos back in the envelope and examined the document. It was headed "Indenture," followed by a description of land. The description referenced a lakeshore and an old stone bridge that could be the bridge to the west of the inn.

Indenture? She'd heard of indentured servitude, but not indentured land.

She replaced the document in the envelope, placed the envelope in the box, picked up the box and headed downstairs. Maybe Dad would know what the document meant.

———

THE NEXT MORNING, Tabby headed downstairs with the indenture document and the box of receipts she'd rescued from Gran's desk. Clattering in the kitchen said he was already downstairs, despite arriving home late last night, after Tabby had gone to bed.

"Dad, what's this?" Tabby unfolded the parchment and placed it on the kitchen counter, next to his coffee, where his newspaper would have been before he made the switch to digital.

He picked up his coffee with one hand and the parchment with the other. "It's a property deed," he said. "Where did you find it?"

"In the writing desk in Gran's room." Tabby prepared her morning latte, then sat opposite her father.

He put his coffee back on the counter, off to the side. "It's not the deed to the inn. That's in the safe in my office."

"The name on the deed—Edwards. Wasn't that Gran's mother's maiden name?"

"It was, so the deed is probably for a property owned by Martha's parents." He turned the paper over again. "It's dated 1912, which fits."

"What's the deed for?"

"You can see the description of the land here." He pointed to a paragraph of text, text so dense it was almost unreadable. "It's describing a large plot of lakefront land, but I don't recognize the name of the lake. Maybe it's the original name of the lake, before the Wainscott family arrived and renamed everything."

"Lake Wainscott or the other lake?" Trinity Lakes Summer Camp was built on a lake that was officially called Lake Other. The triplets had long ago decided "Lake Other" was a stupid name, so they always referred to it as the other lake.

"It could be Lake Wainscott." He turned the paper upside down, as though a different perspective would make the location clearer. "Was there anything with this? A map, maybe?"

"Just two old photos. One of the boat shed, and one that looked like Great-grandmother's wedding photograph."

"The boat shed? That would suggest the deed is for part of the shore of Lake Wainscott, possibly the land in front of us. I wonder . . ." He pulled out his phone and took a photo of the deed. "The boat shed is owned by some secret trust that pays the property tax and nothing else."

"How do you know that?" Tabby gave him a sideways look.

"The council is trying to figure out who owns the boat shed so they can force them to tidy the place up. I had an official visit from the mayor to ask if any of my clients were behind the secret trust."

"And?"

"And I told him he was asking the wrong person. Mind you, I wouldn't be able to tell him even if I knew."

Tabby picked up the deed. "What should I do with this?"

"We need to find out if it's a valid current deed, and what property it's for."

"Morning, Tabby. Mr. Thomas. What's cooking?" Logan arrived in the kitchen with more energy than should be possible while wearing a walking boot. His ankle must be improving.

"We have a mystery," Dad said. "Do you know anything about property deeds? Or inheritance law?"

"I know how to read a property deed, but that's all." Logan took a seat at the kitchen counter. "As for inheritance law? Trent's the law student, not me."

What was Logan's area of expertise? She'd assumed it was partying and perpetually playing tourist.

Dad pushed the deed over the counter to Logan. "Maybe this is something you could help Tabby investigate."

"Sure." Logan picked up the document. "What am I looking at?"

"A property deed I found in Gran's room. But we don't know what property." Tabby passed over the photograph of the boat shed. "I found this as well."

"Could it be the deed for the boat shed?" Logan asked. "Although the description seems to cover a bigger piece of land."

"If the deed is for the boat shed, does that mean Gran owned it? And that we own it now?" Tabby asked.

"It's possible," Dad said. "We'd need to check the county records." Dad turned to Logan. "When Grace died, Martha changed her will to leave her estate in trust for her three grand-children, Tabitha, Tiffany, and Trent."

"Grace was your mother, right?"

Tabby nodded. "Wait. What? We own the inn? Me and Tiffy and Trent?"

"Of course you do. I thought you knew that."

"Does that mean we can sell the inn? Not that I want to, but —" But Trent and Tiffy were always complaining that college was expensive, complaining that they'd be crippled by student loans by the time they graduated. If Trent and Tiffy knew they could sell the inn . . .

"No. The assets are all held in trust until you're twenty-five. Then you can sell the property if you all agree to the sale. Otherwise, it remains in trust and you each receive an equal portion of the income."

"So if Gran legally owned the property indicated in this deed, that would be part of the trust?"

"That's my understanding, yes," Dad said. "But first we'd need to confirm what the deed is for—if it's the boat shed or something else—and if she still owned it. It's possible this is an old deed, and the land was sold years ago."

"How would we do that?"

"Land ownership is a matter of public record." Dad took a sip of coffee. "Find out where the property is and what records the city has about current or past owners. Assuming Martha owned the property, it would have been transferred to the trust. The best person to ask is her lawyer."

"I don't have time." Tabby had enough to do already. She didn't need anything else added to her overflowing plate.

"I have plenty of time," Logan said. "Where do I start?"

"The lawyer wouldn't be able to tell you anything—you're not the owner or beneficiary or their legal representative—but you could do some of the background research."

"Would you mind?" Should she take him up on his offer? It

was one thing to accept his help with the inn. It was another to accept his help on family business.

"I've already binge-watched too much Netflix, and my physio—sorry, PT—would probably appreciate me doing something low-impact like desk research. It's this or doomscrolling social media."

"Let him help, Tabby." Dad looked at her with raised eyebrows, as if he knew she wanted to say no even though she needed the help.

Gran had always drummed into her the importance of graciously accepting help when offered. Besides, Logan's helping would give her more excuses to spend time with him. Not that she needed excuses. And not that she should be wanting to spend time with him, given there was no way they could have a relationship beyond friendship . . . as she had to keep reminding herself.

"If you're sure." Her smile felt shaky. "Thank you."

CHAPTER SIX

"Good morning, Logan. Did you sleep well?" Tabitha asked as he hobbled into the kitchen.

Her greeting would have been a bit too cheery if it wasn't for the fact that he'd had an excellent night's sleep. The rest and fresh lakeside air over the last two weeks were doing their job. Tabitha looked more relaxed and rested herself and had regained some of the bounce he remembered from previous visits. Her increased energy was great to see, and only made her more attractive.

Wait. This was Tabitha, Trent's sister. The woman the bro code said he couldn't pursue.

"Good, thank you. Is there anything I can do?" Tabitha bustled beside the stove, flipping what looked like pancakes. They'd set the table last night, but he didn't want to sit and watch her work if he could help.

"All under control, thanks." She flipped a cooked pancake out of the pan and onto a plate, then added more butter to the pan and swirled in a scoop of batter. "What can I get you for breakfast?"

"I'm good with muesli."

"Muesli?" She turned to look at him, and he held up a jar half-filled with what looked like homemade muesli. "Oh, you mean granola. Help yourself."

"Thanks." Logan heaped muesli into a bowl, added the milk, then perched himself on one of the stools under the wide kitchen counter. "This is good. Homemade?"

"Of course."

"What time will the guests come down for breakfast this morning?"

Tabitha looked at the clock. Seven thirty. "One room has booked for eight, and the other two for nine."

"Then I'll eat quickly and get out of your way before they show up."

"Any plans for the day?" Tabitha slid another pancake onto the plate and started the process again.

"I was going to see if I could find anything online about that deed you found in your Gran's desk." It was good to have things to do—sedentary things. Otherwise, he'd be tempted to do something stupid like ask Tabitha if she'd like to go for a walk along the lakefront.

"That would be great." She looked as though she had the weight of the world on her slim shoulders . . . again.

"I can help with the guest rooms this morning if you want. Or help with your Gran's suite." He could surf the internet anytime.

"No one's checking out today, so there won't be much to do in the rooms today."

"Would you like me to make the beds and change the towels while they're having breakfast?" He was pleased with how his ankle was healing, so a few trips up and down the stairs wouldn't hurt. "Then I can help you in Martha's room."

"Could you?" Was she now standing straighter, or was that merely his imagination?

Two hours later, they were back in Martha's living room.

Last week, Logan's impression had been that the suite was over-stuffed. His second visit reinforced that first impression. Over-stuffed with furniture, with books, with knickknacks, with a lifetime of memories. Good memories. Memories that should be kept and cherished, not consigned to the metaphorical or physical trash can. No wonder Tabitha had been procrastinating about clearing it out.

Worse, none of it coordinated with the decor downstairs. The guest rooms and public areas of the inn were decorated in a classy minimalist style, with an emphasis on quality decor and furnishings. Not this overstuffed hotchpotch of objects in a range of styles and colors with no unifying theme. Great. Now he sounded like his interior designer mother.

"We did a good job with the kitchen," Logan said. "Where would you like to start this morning?"

"Where do you think?" She clearly had no idea where to start.

Logan slowly turned, taking in the whole room. Martha had obviously been a keen reader, because there were books every-where. "How about we start with the books?"

"Books. Okay."

"Have you had any thoughts on what you'll do with them?"

"There's some space in the library downstairs."

"How much space?" He had no idea, as he tended to avoid the guest areas except when he was helping clean.

"Not enough. We can't possibly keep them all." Again, she seemed to deflate as she spoke.

"So we start by sorting them." He did his best to keep his tone positive, upbeat, in an attempt to encourage her. "Do you have a local library or church library we could donate to?"

"The public library might be interested if they're in good condition. Or a church library, if they're Christian titles."

"Or a book sale? Back home, a couple of charities run annual secondhand book sales as fundraisers. They're always looking for good quality donations." Although he doubted these books fit the "good quality" criteria. There was a distinct smell of mildew hanging around the room, with old paperbacks the likely culprit.

"There aren't any local book sales."

"So let's go through them one stack at a time. Look at each book and decide if it's something you want to keep, donate, or throw away."

"We can't throw away books. It's . . . wrong." Tabitha looked as though he'd just suggested she sacrifice her firstborn child.

"In general, I agree with you." Logan did his best to keep his tone neutral and dispassionate, to appeal to Tabitha's logical side. "But this room has a mildewy smell, so I'm guessing some of these books have mold. Throwing them away might be the only option." He picked up a novel with an illustrated cover decades out of date and held it toward her. "Look." Half the back cover had been eaten away by who knew what.

"Book mites. Eww." Tabitha took the book from him and turned it back over. "I didn't know Gran read romance novels."

"We need some boxes," Logan said. He was not going to get into a conversation with Tabitha about romance novels . . . not unless there was a chance it might lead to a conversation with Tabitha about actual romance. Not something that was on the cards, if he was reading her right. But was he? He could swear there were times over the last two weeks when she'd looked at him with what could have been interest. Or maybe that was his imagination, and he was misreading her cues.

"I'll run down and grab some of Dad's archive boxes." Tabitha replaced the novel in the pile and left the room.

Logan made a start on sorting the books, inspecting them for mold or mildew or mites, and checking the inside cover to see if there were inscriptions or anything to indicate the book had some sentimental significance. Most had nothing but a scribbled-out name, suggesting they'd been purchased secondhand. Some were old library books, and he doubted the library would want them back.

He'd only got through a small stack before Tabitha returned with three flat-pack boxes.

"Let me help." His many moves during his childhood and teenage years had given him plenty of experience in assembling packing boxes, and he made quick work of the task. "How do you want to sort the books?"

"As much as I don't want to throw books away, anything that's got book mites or mold or mildew or isn't good enough to donate will have to go in the trash. The rest can get divided up between the public library, the church library, and the inn library."

"You probably know what books you have downstairs better than me, so how about I check to see if a book is worth keeping or donating, and you can figure out where the good ones should go."

"Sounds like a plan."

———

Now Tabby had started, going through Gran's endless book collection wasn't as difficult as she'd feared. Most of them seemed to be romance novels, which was unexpected but not surprising. Gran—and many of the other older ladies in town— had a penchant for what they called matchmaking, and what Tiffy and Trent called meddling.

She flicked open a random novel, *Search for Tomorrow* by Mary Hawkins. An Australian author—interesting. There was a series list at the back of the novel, which Tabby compared with the books on the shelf. How funny. Gran, who "organized" her financial affairs by throwing her receipts in an old shoebox, had shelved the series in order of publication.

Most of the books were in relatively good condition. She

could list them on eBay. Maybe someone out there would be interested in what looked like every Heartsong Presents novel published in the last century.

Tabby took photos of all the book spines on the shelf, and another of the book in her hand. Trent wouldn't be interested in any of these titles, and Tiffy probably wouldn't either, but she'd give them the option before deciding where to donate them.

She texted both photos to her siblings.

Do either of you want any of these books? If not, we'll donate them or sell them on eBay.

"We" would mean her, as it did with anything to do with the inn. She'd find the time. Somehow.

She set the book aside and moved the rest of the series into an archive box, making sure to keep them in order, while Logan pulled down books from the higher shelves.

Ding. A message from Trent.

I don't want any of them.

No surprise there. And she didn't expect Tiffy to answer any time soon—between med school lectures and study, Tiffy barely had time to eat. Trent wasn't much better. He'd decided to go to law school, which was going to take another two years and who knew how many thousand dollars. At least he'd managed to secure a paid internship with a prominent Seattle law firm. He still claimed he didn't have any money, but he somehow seemed to have plenty of free time, because he always answered her infrequent texts immediately.

An hour later, they had two large bags of books to trash or recycle—Tabby couldn't remember if Trinity Lakes had a paper recycling depot, but maybe one of the crafty ladies at the Main Street Emporium would know. She also had one box to shelve in the guest library downstairs, and two boxes for the church or public library. Tabby had kept a couple of books aside for senti-mental reasons—Gran's Bible for herself, and a century-old Book of Common Prayer with an inscription showing it first belonged to their great-grandmother, Rose. Tabby would offer that to Tiffy.

Tabby checked her phone—not even lunchtime yet. Great, because that meant she had time to have a quick look at the stack of photo albums she'd removed from the desk.

She picked up the first album and opened it to the front page. It was a picture of her parents on their wedding day. She hadn't seen the photo before, but she recognized them. Dad looked much the same now as in the photo, just thirty years older. Mom? Well, Mom looked like Tabby and Tiffy. Or Tiffy and Tabby looked like Mom. She showed Logan the photograph.

"You look like your mother," Logan said from over her shoulder.

"I know. She was only twenty-four when she died, so she's probably about my age in this photo." Tabby brushed her hand over the photo, as if touching the photo would be like touching her mother. Their mother had died when the triplets were less than a week old, not old enough to have even an echo of a memory.

"Do you want to keep looking?" Logan asked.

Tabby closed her eyes and took a deep breath in an effort to control her emotions and not collapse into a bundle of tears. "I think I'd just like to look through this album."

She turned and moved to the overstuffed loveseat, now clear of books and debris, and sat down. These pictures were a precious insight into her mother's life, and a reminder of how much Gran and Dad and the triplets had lost when she died. Logan took a seat by her side, a comforting presence as she leafed through the pages, lost in thoughts of what might have been.

CHAPTER SEVEN

"Where would you like these?" Logan lifted a half-full box of books and looked over the top at Tabby. It had taken two days, but they finally had all the books sorted.

"Those are the books I want to keep, so they can go to my bedroom. But should you be carrying them?" she asked.

"I'll be fine. My ankle's feeling a lot better." Thanks, no doubt, to a couple of weeks of doing practically nothing except the exercises the physio had prescribed, reading, and surfing the internet. "And your room is only next door. It's not like I'm going to trip down the stairs."

The room Tabitha had once shared with Tiffany was next to the Grandma suite, opposite Trent's room. He pushed open the door with his foot, sided in, and placed the box on the floor next to one of the beds.

He leaned down to massage his ankle. Fine, as he'd expected, even though he'd taken off the moon boot. Walking in a straight line was no trouble.

As he straightened, a flash of color on the bedroom wall caught his eye. A postcard of the Trevi Fountain in Rome.

Was that the postcard he'd sent Trent the summer he'd

visited his parents in Italy? The postcard was tacked to a cork-board, so he carefully removed it, looked at the back, and found his own handwriting. That was . . . unexpected.

He replaced the postcard on the board and stepped back. The corkboard was covered with postcards from all over the world, many from places he'd visited. He recognized a couple as joke postcards he'd sent Trent. Others were vintage postcards—he could tell from the cars and the clothing. Tabitha didn't seem like the kind of person to collect vintage postcards, so who had sent those?

Footsteps sounded outside, and Tabby lurched into the room with another full box.

"Hey, let me help with that."

"This one's light—it's just a few of her handmade throw cushions. I left the box of photo albums for you."

"Good." He didn't want her moving heavy boxes, not if he was around. "What's with the postcards? I remember sending Trent that picture of the Trevi Fountain."

"You've sent a few to Trent."

"I think they're all up here." Logan tried to hide his curiosity. Why had she kept the postcards? Was it because he'd sent them? Or was it because of the places they portrayed? He'd prefer the former, but the latter was more likely.

"It's kind of a collection."

He'd guessed that. "Where did you get the others?" He motioned toward the corkboard. "Some of those are really old."

"The vintage ones were postcards Gran collected when she and Grandad did a big European tour on their honeymoon. They bought postcards wherever they visited but didn't send them."

"My parents and grandparents did that—in the days before digital cameras, they'd buy a couple of postcards so they had a memento of the places they'd visited, in case their own photographs didn't turn out."

"It's hard to imagine life before digital cameras or the internet."

"Isn't that the truth." Logan had never owned a proper camera. He always traveled light, so he'd relied on his mobile phone for photos and rarely bought souvenirs for himself—not even postcards. That made traveling easier, but it did mean he had almost nothing to show for the last three years of his life. Nothing physical, at least. "Why did you keep them?"

"Memories." She paused, as though reflecting. "Gran used to talk about her trips with Grandad. They went everywhere— Egypt, Israel, Rome, Paris. Even Japan and India. All sorts of places."

All places he'd been.

"Places you'd like to go?" It was a guess, but there was something about the way she stood, hands on hips, gazing at the corkboard as though she was looking through the pictures to the places they showed.

"Yes." The word was almost a whisper. "I'd like to travel, to see the world. But . . ."

"There's nothing stopping you." She was young, free, with no family ties to keep her in Trinity Lakes.

"There's everything stopping me. Dad. The inn. My job."

Logan raised his eyebrows. Her father wouldn't stop her. The inn could hire a cook and cleaner. Hannah could find a new assistant manager.

The only thing stopping Tabitha was Tabitha herself.

Tabitha had rarely left Trinity Lakes, but that wasn't because she didn't want to leave. Was it because she believed she couldn't leave?

If she secretly wanted to travel . . .

Maybe they weren't as different as he'd assumed. That thought opened a world of happy possibilities.

"WHAT DID YOU DO TODAY?" Tabby asked as she and Logan took their seats on the front veranda the following evening. This was turning into a habit. A good habit, one she enjoyed. Did she enjoy it because she was taking time to relax? Or because it was an excuse to spend alone time with Logan? That wasn't a question she wanted to explore.

"Did my PT exercises. Went to the gym. Visited the city offices."

"The city offices? About the deed? Weren't you going to search online?"

"There wasn't much information online, so I visited the city offices."

"Did you find anything?"

"From what I've been able to work out from the official records, the first registered owner of the lakefront land was Isaiah Wainscott. He deeded the land directly in front of the inn into a trust, designating it as community land—clever, because it means no one can build there."

"What about the land between here and the rowing club? That's all part of Hannah's family trust."

"That's a little more difficult to trace. I found the current deed, which shows the land is currently owned by the Gilbertson Family Trust—I assume that's Hannah's family?"

"That's right."

"I also found that all the lakefront land is zoned as a floodplain."

"What does that mean?" Had Hannah mentioned something about a floodplain?

"It should mean the land is liable to flood, which has development and insurance implications. But I couldn't find any record of the rationale for the zoning. That's . . . unusual."

"Why is it unusual?"

"There should be an engineer's report detailing why the land has been zoned as a floodplain. And the zoning doesn't make sense. Most floodplains are flat areas to the side of rivers."

Tabby waved her arm to the side, as though she was a circus ringmaster introducing the main act. "Lake Wainscott. Trinity Lakes. Trinity River."

Logan waved his arm behind them in an equally elegant flourish. "Hills. Mountains. No open plains."

"What about that?" Tabby gestured toward the old boat shed, park, sailing club, and the rowing club. "That's flat."

"It's a lakefront. A lakefront is geographically different from a floodplain."

"Are you saying floodplains are never near lakes?"

"Not never. Some rivers change course and leave a small lake where the river used to be. That can be a floodplain. But most land designated as a floodplain used to be a river. Not because it's a lake."

"There must be a reason why the lakefront has been zoned as a floodplain."

"A reason? Probably. A geographical reason?" Logan stood, hands on hips, gazing across the lake. "It doesn't fit. Unless the lake has a history of flooding."

"How would we find that out?"

"I'll do some more research." He offered Tabby his wry smile, the smile that never failed to steal the breath from her lungs.

———

IN THE LAST WEEK, Tabby and Logan had completely cleared Gran's bathroom and bookshelves. Now Tabby had decided it was time to start on the bedroom—the most important task if her goal was to renovate the room ready for guests.

This was going to be harder than the bookshelves, but it was time to start.

"Logan, can you strip the bed, please?" The sheets were clean

—she'd changed them when Gran was admitted to hospital that last time, even though they hadn't known it was going to be the last time. But removing Gran's faded flannel sheets in her favorite fuchsia floral pattern one final time was one final reminder that Gran was gone and wouldn't be returning.

"Sure."

"I'll start on the bathroom." But not before she'd stopped and taken a second to admire the view of a man stripping a bed.

And not just any man.

Logan.

Contrary to the promise of the old saying, familiarity was not breeding contempt, in the same way as out of sight had not been out of mind. The more time she spent with him, the more she liked and respected him.

And he seemed to like her as well. Awkward, because he was still wrong for her.

She headed into the bathroom. She should get to work and be grateful she had help. Not spend her time wishing for what might have been with the help, if the help had been Christian.

Fortunately, clearing out the bathroom shouldn't be any harder than clearing out Gran's kitchen. The harder task would be figuring out what to do with Gran's clothes and personal possessions, and how to redecorate.

"Hey, Tabby," Logan called from the bedroom. "Have you looked under the bed?"

"No." Tabby stood from where she was emptying the bathroom cupboard and leaned against the bedroom door frame. "I didn't realize there was anything under the bed. What have you found?"

"Enough dust to start a garden, and a lot of boxes. Do you want to take a look?"

"Okay."

He pulled out the first box, which rattled.

"Oops. I hope I haven't broken anything."

Tabby crouched beside him. There were no markings on the box, nothing to indicate what was inside. A single strip of yellowed packing tape held the box closed.

"Do you want to do the honors?" Logan asked.

Her confusion must have shown on her face.

"Do you want to open it?" he asked.

No. Yes. She pulled at the packing tape. It came away easily, having long since lost any adhesive quality. She opened the box to find stacks of bone china crockery in a range of floral patterns. Cups, saucers, plates, milk jugs, sugar bowls, even a teapot.

Logan pulled out a cup and turned it over. "Royal Albert Old Country Roses. My grandmother's favorite pattern."

Tabby picked up two more cups. "This one is Royal Albert as well—Lavender Rose. And this says Royal Albert, but nothing else."

Logan pulled another box out from under the bed, more carefully this time.

"This one's heavier. I don't think it's china."

The packing tape was just as old and stripped off just as easily. Tabby opened the box to find two neat piles of what looked like scrapbooks. Not the fancy modern kind, full of Pinterest-perfect photo arrangements and embellishments, but the old-fashioned kind, cheap cardboard covers with newsprint pages.

She took the top scrapbook out of the box. Its profile was curved from what must be layers and layers of paper stuck inside. She opened the album to the first page, which showed two photographs of the boat shed. One was a black-and-white photograph printed on newsprint, which looked as though it had been cut out of the newspaper. The picture was a little blurry, typical of old newspaper photos she'd seen from back before they introduced digital printing, and showed the boat shed as it must have looked when it was new. The second was a washed-out color photograph of the boat shed in disrepair.

Logan swiveled around the box to look at the photos with her. "Interesting. That's obviously an old photograph, but the boat shed looks even worse than it does now. Someone must have done some repairs and given it a coat of paint since this was taken."

Tabby looked again, more carefully this time. Logan was right. The photograph showed rotting boards, peeling paint, and boarded-up windows. She turned the page. The two-page spread showed a hand-drawn floor plan of a rectangular-shaped building with a kitchen and bathrooms clearly marked.

She flicked through the next few pages to find someone's carefully arranged color choices and room layouts. There were paint swatches—the kind people pick up from the hardware store—with half a dozen colors circled in red marker pen. There were pages and pages of color photos cut from glossy magazines, pictures of tablecloths and table settings, crockery and cutlery, carpets, and curtains.

Some pages had handwritten notes pointing to parts of a picture, saying "this" or "look here." Toward the middle were pictures of commercial kitchens, all gleaming stainless steel. And more notes. The last pages were blank, but there was a large envelope tucked inside the back cover. Tabby opened the flap and looked inside.

"I guess this is the stuff she hadn't yet stuck in the scrapbook." Tabby reached inside and pulled out a handful of paper.

"Those look like quotes from contractors." Logan held out his hand, and Tabby passed over the pile of paper. "Yes, definitely quotes."

"Quotes for what?"

"Building repair and renovation. This one's for repairing and repainting the exterior." He passed a stapled handful of paper back to Tabby. "This one is for manufacture and installation of a kitchen."

"But what's it all for?" Tabby asked, not expecting an answer.

"Can you go back to the first page of the scrapbook?" Logan asked. "The double page with what looked like a building blueprint."

She turned back, and Logan examined the page more closely.

"I think this is the blueprint for the boat shed," he said. "The ratios and dimensions are right, and the windows and doors are in the same places." He indicated what looked like narrow boxes on the sides of the larger rectangle. "These are the windows, and this is the main door."

Tabby flicked back to the very front page, the page with the photographs, then back to the drawing. Logan was right.

"So if this is the boat shed, all these other pictures are Gran's plans for renovating it and turning it into some kind of event venue."

"That would be my guess."

"What's the crockery for? It's all different patterns. An event venue would want everything to be in a single pattern." At least, that was her experience.

"There're three or four more boxes under the bed. They might have an answer."

Logan dragged out the remaining boxes and opened them. One held more unmatched bone china cups and saucers. One held larger plates, again in a range of brands and patterns but all genuine English bone china, all neatly wrapped in tissue paper. Another held tarnished silver cutlery in a range of patterns, but no answers to her questions.

"I don't want to be the person who gets to polish all this," Tabby said.

"Can't you buy some kind of silver polish dip?" Logan asked. "The kind jewelers use? That would be easier."

"Then I'd have to keep it polished."

"Or use it. I remember my grandmother saying silver doesn't need to be polished if it's used all the time." Logan shrugged.

"It would need to be washed by hand. No thanks." She had enough to do without washing and drying cutlery by hand.

Tabby pulled the packing tape back on the final box and opened it. It held half a dozen bone china teapots in patterns which matched the cups, saucers, and plates, along with some cake platters.

"Gran often talked about wanting to have a café or something where she could serve high tea in the afternoon—cucumber sandwiches and scones and petit fours. All the fancy stuff."

"Sounds very *Downton Abbey.*"

"You watched *Downton Abbey?*" This was a new side to Logan's character.

"My grandmother watched *Downton Abbey*. She'd tell me all about it in our weekly video calls."

Gran had been a big fan of the acerbic wit of Violet Crawley, the Dowager Countess played by Dame Maggie Smith, although Tabby had always preferred Lady Sybil. She admired Lady Sybil's courage and determination in going after what she wanted . . . what Gran called Lady Sybil's rebellious streak.

"So maybe the scrapbook was Gran's plan for bringing a little English class to Trinity Lakes. I wonder why she didn't do it." She had the designs, the plans, the quotes. "Maybe she didn't have the money."

"Or maybe there was another reason." Logan busied himself replacing the papers in the envelope and repacking the boxes in a way that looked like he was avoiding her question.

"Like what?" Maybe she should channel a little of the rebellious Lady Sybil instead of being the respectable, responsible sister. "Logan. Why do you think Gran didn't do it?"

"The quotes are dated 1999, and I'm guessing that's when the scrapbooks were put together."

"You think Gran gave up on her dream because of us? Because Mom died and Dad moved us all into the inn?"

"It would make sense. She wouldn't have had time, not while she was looking after three newborn babies."

"But what about when we were older?"

"Maybe her dream died. Or changed. Maybe it wasn't her calling."

Gran had always said her calling was to raise her family to love God and serve others. Tabby was doing her best to honor Gran by following her example.

What had Gran given up to raise Tabby and Tiffy and Trent, her second family?

What if that hadn't been Gran's dream?

CHAPTER EIGHT

Two months in Trinity Lakes hadn't been Logan's plan, but he had to admit he was enjoying his time here. Today he'd do some more investigation into the boat shed, chasing down any number of online rabbit holes, run through his ankle exercises, and head to the gym to do some weights and get a physical therapist-approved cardio workout on the stationary bikes or the rowing machine. He needed to keep his cardio fitness up if he was going to spend the summer chasing teens around camp.

He'd love to get out and run along the lakefront boardwalk, but not until he was confident his ankle could take the workout. He'd even rented a kayak one Friday morning and explored the lake while Tabby was busy in the inn.

Kayaking was a good upper body and aerobic workout that was physio-approved because it didn't use his ankle. He'd found a secluded beach that would make a great picnic spot for a romantic date . . . if he ever summoned up courage. Tabitha was friendly and welcoming and had accepted a couple of hugs when she'd been upset, but the way she actively avoided touching him said she wasn't interested.

His research on the boat shed was going better and worse than expected. He'd confirmed the triplets did own the boat shed—at least, the boat shed was owned by the same trust as the inn. He hadn't been able to talk to Martha's lawyer—as expected, she would only talk to the trustees or the beneficiaries —but he had found out a lot about floodplains. Not the "what is a floodplain?" kind of information he'd studied in college, but the implications of land being zoned as a floodplain.

And there were a lot.

Tabitha had said clearing out and renovating the Grandma flat would be difficult. That task had nothing on the red tape required to renovate the boat shed.

The one glimmer of light and hope was that it did seem possible to get the land rezoned—they would need to commission an official engineering report from a registered surveyor or engineer.

First, he needed to find out if there was any known history of flooding. And that meant talking to Tabitha.

He could hear her clattering in the kitchen downstairs. No doubt she was busy cooking or baking for the family, the guests, or some church event.

That was something he'd noticed in the time he'd been here —Tabitha was always on the go. She was going to burn out if she wasn't careful. Some people thought burnout was the privilege of the rich—highly paid workaholics who worked more hours in a week than should be humanly possible.

But burnout was also a problem for the poor—the people who worked two or three jobs to feed their families. Tabitha didn't fit in that category either, yet she was always working, always serving, never resting . . . except in the evenings when he was able to persuade her to take a break with him on the veranda.

He headed downstairs to the kitchen, where Tabitha looked like she was baking a cake.

"I've found out more about the boat shed."

Tabitha looked up from measuring cups of flour and gave him a warm smile. "Good news?"

"Not so much, I'm afraid. The land is zoned as a floodplain, and that means there are implications for what work can be done and how. Your best option would be to get the zoning changed."

Tabitha cracked an egg into the mixture. "What?"

Logan turned his iPad toward her. "If the boat shed is zoned as a floodplain, you'll need to get the zoning changed. Otherwise, you'll need a special Floodplain Development Permit before you can do any work."

"Where do we get that? From the city? And how much does it cost?" She rested the beater on the counter and wiped her hands on her apron.

"Yes, from the city, but it doesn't say how much it costs. But that's not all. If you're borrowing money for the work, you'll need flood insurance. That could get expensive."

"Why?"

"It's based on how high the property is above the hundred-year floodplain. The boat shed is only a couple of meters—six feet—above the lake, so I'm guessing the floodplain is much higher."

"That doesn't sound good." Tabitha picked up the iPad and scrolled through the information on the screen. "This says we can appeal the floodplain designation. We just have to hire a surveyor or engineer to say the land isn't on a floodplain."

"A surveyor or engineer is only going to say that if it's true."

"I've lived here my whole life, and the lake has never come any higher than it is right now." Tabitha reached into a large drawer and clattered about.

"It's the hundred-year flood zone. Technically, it's the one percent flood zone—the point at which there is a one percent chance of flooding each year."

"Gran lived in Trinity Lakes for her entire life and never mentioned floods." Tabby paused, as if mentally reviewing a lifetime of conversations with her grandmother. "She did say the river has burst its banks a couple of times."

That could be important. "How high did the water get?"

"I think the trailer park might have flooded." She arranged four muffin tins on the counter, then picked up a box of cupcake papers. "But nothing major—it was inches of water, not feet. That's why they put the trailer park there, not houses."

That wasn't good, but it also wasn't note-it-on-the-property-deed bad. "Are there stories about the lake flooding? My grandmother used to live in a town that was built on a floodplain between three rivers. She had stories about a flood back in the sixties, when she was a child. Adults were wading through chest-high water. Did your grandmother have any stories like that?"

"No." Tabitha didn't pause from adding the cupcake papers to the muffin tins. "None."

"Did she ever mention the rivers breaking their banks, or the lake water coming up high?"

"How high?" She picked up the bowl she'd been stirring and started spooning the mixture into the muffin tins.

"Say . . . as high as the carpark. High enough for water to get into the boat shed."

"Not that I can remember. Dad might know more, although he only moved here when we were born, so he won't know anything before that."

"So we might be able to do some research and find out."

She stopped spooning. "How do you know so much about this stuff? I thought you studied sports science."

Or some other dropout subject. She didn't say it. She didn't have to. He'd heard it before—from his parents, from his classmates, from family and friends and colleagues.

"Social science with a geography major and a business

minor." Not what his father called a real degree, but one that served as an entry point for a variety of careers. Which would be useful if Logan had any idea what career he wanted . . .

"So that's how you know about stuff like floodplains."

"Also, my dad's an architect. He mostly works on new builds, but he's done a few projects where he had to find a way to integrate protected historic buildings with the new and functional." That, combined with several summers as a laborer on various building sites had given Logan a broad understanding of a lot of topics around construction. "So Lake Wainscott hasn't ever flooded. What about the other two lakes?"

"Not that I know of. Not that Gran ever mentioned."

"That sounds promising." Logan tap-tap-tapped his fingers on the countertop. "If there had been floods, they would have been news."

"Like photos in the local newspaper and stuff?" Tabitha resumed spooning muffin mixture into the tins.

"I could have a look through the archives," Logan said. "How old is your town newspaper, and how often does it get published?"

"It's weekly. I think it started in the 1880s, but I could be wrong. I think the library has old issues of the newspaper." She replaced the bowl on the counter, loaded the filled muffin tins into the oven, and set the timer.

"Then I'll visit the library on Monday and see if I can find anything."

"The librarian, Mr. Masters, knows everyone and everything about Trinity Lakes. If there's been a major flood, he'd know." Tabitha opened the dishwasher and started stacking dirty dishes.

"If I find pictures of the lake in flood, we'd have evidence to say the lake is a floodplain. But the reverse isn't true."

"Not finding photographs won't prove the lake isn't a floodplain." She tapped her chin with a finger.

"It could mean the lake isn't a floodplain. But it could just be that there aren't any pictures of the lake in flood."

"Surely someone would have taken a photograph if the lake flooded." She closed the dishwasher.

"You'd think so, but it might depend on how bad the flood was. Or when."

It was going to be a whole lot easier to prove there was a problem than to prove there wasn't.

LOGAN CRANKED open the door to the town library and found himself in a room slightly larger than the boat shed. The space was dominated by dozens of dark wooden bookshelves, which wore the patina of a hundred years. To his left sat an old wooden desk with a high front, bare except for a small stainless steel bell. Narrow stairs to his right led to who knew where. The room was empty, so he rang the bell. The sound echoed in the empty room, and feet appeared at the top of the stairs.

"Who are you and what do you want?" The speaker was a man with a beard to rival any mall Santa, and the hair to match. There the resemblance ended. This man hadn't eaten nearly as many Christmas treats as the typical Santa, nor did he have Santa's famous red cheeks.

"My name is Logan Wylde. I'm staying at the Lakeview Inn, and I'm looking into the history of the area and the property. Tabitha told me you keep old issues of the newspaper here."

"I do." The man's tone was a long way from friendly.

"I was hoping I could take a look. If that's all right." Logan adopted his politest tone and hammed up his accent a little. Most Americans responded well to his Kiwi accent, but there were always exceptions.

"You're supposed to call ahead and make an appointment." The man moved behind the desk and opened a drawer.

"Sorry. I can come back another day if that's more convenient." Logan gave a bright smile he hoped was conciliatory.

"Do you know how to use a microfiche reader?"

"Yes, sir."

"You're staying at Lakeview, you say. Do you know the Thomases?"

"Trent and I were roommates in college."

"I used to play bridge with Martha, God rest her soul. Martha used to tell us about Trent and his college escapades. Name's Masters. William Masters."

"A pleasure to meet you, Mr. Masters." What college stories had the man heard? Logan's stories were tamer than Trent's, but Logan wouldn't be the one to reveal that.

"Follow me." The man headed up the stairs he'd come down, crossed another book-filled room, then ushered Logan up another, narrower flight of stairs.

"I've been helping Tabitha sort through Martha's bookshelves. Would the library be interested in any donations?"

"Of Martha's books? I doubt it. Watch your step."

They emerged into the attic, which was filled with filing cabinets of various sizes, and a few large flat desks in the center, large enough to read a broadsheet. One desk held an aged microfiche reader. The furniture was a mix of old and older. Nothing matched, and nothing looked as though it was made in this century.

In fact, the only modern thing in the room was the air conditioning system.

William Masters closed the door behind them. "Keep the door shut," he said. "Whole room is climate controlled—light, temperature, humidity. We've got over one hundred forty years of history here, and I don't want it spoiled by some idiot who doesn't know how to close the door behind himself. Although Martha never said you were an idiot. That grandson of hers? Now, he was another subject."

"No, sir." Or should he have said, "Yes, sir"?

"Here's the microfiche. Turn it off when you're not using it, or else it overheats."

"I imagine machines like these are difficult to replace," Logan said.

"Impossible. We have all the original newspapers and the microfiche copies. I'd like to get everything digitized as a backup, but the city won't give me funding."

"How long would it take to digitize the archive?" Logan asked.

"It's not the scanning that's the issue. It's the indexing—making the archive searchable."

"So people can find articles on a specific topic." Rather than trawling through acres of papers, as it sounded like Logan would have to do.

"Correct," faux Santa said. "Are you looking for something specific?"

Good question. Logan didn't want to tell him he was specifically investigating the history of flooding in the area in case word got back to the council or town planner or whoever was behind the zoning. That could make things difficult for Tabitha and her family.

But he also didn't want to say he wasn't looking for anything in particular. In his limited experience, librarians and archivists were happy to help as long as their customers knew what they were looking for. They were a lot less ready to help informational sightseers search for needles in proverbial haystacks.

"I'd like to look into the history of the inn and the surrounding land," he said. "Tabitha is thinking of redecorating her grandmother's rooms—"

"I'm sure they need it," Mr. Masters said.

"Tabitha has a lot of ideas, but she'd like the room to be a testament to her grandmother's memory. She doesn't know a lot about her grandmother's early years, except that her parents or grandparents built the inn, so we hoped there might be something here to give us inspiration."

"I suppose she's too busy to come herself," the man said. Logan was about to jump to her defense when Mr. Masters went on, his tone noticeably softer. "That girl does too much. Always here and there, to-ing and fro-ing, looking after other people."

"That's what I keep telling her, sir, and that's why I offered to investigate the archive for her. If I can find some information and perhaps some pictures, she can choose what she wants to use."

"If you find any good pictures in the papers, make a note. We may still have the original prints or negatives. Depends on what she's looking for."

"Thank you, sir. I appreciate it."

"Now, let's get you set up." Mr. Masters showed Logan where the different decades of film were stored. "It's all filed by date. Like I said, no money for indexes."

"Can I print from the microfilms?" Logan asked.

"Dollar a page. Printer is over there." He gestured toward the far corner of the room. "I've got work to do. I'll leave you to it."

"Thank you, sir."

Logan picked a random roll of microfiche. 1954. Not a year he was interested in, but he probably should start by looking through a few older issues to see how often the newspaper was printed and what kind of stories it carried. That might give him an idea of the best way to approach his search.

Five hours later, he'd found stories about the building of the house that was now the Lakeview Inn, the building of the boat shed—by the same people who built Lakeview Lodge, as it was then called—and a picture of Tabitha, Trent, and Tiffy with both their parents the day they were born—1 January 2000.

He'd also found several pictures of a flooded river flowing out of Lake Wainscott. What he hadn't found were any photographs of the lake in flood—or photographs of any of the lakes in flood.

He printed off a handful of pictures to show Tabitha, including the baby photo. There were various family photos on display in the house, but he'd never seen this one. Perhaps Mr. Thomas didn't want the reminder, given he lost his wife only a few days later.

A door opened, and Mr. Masters hobbled into the room. "Finished yet, boy? I need to lock up."

"I've finished. Thank you for all your help. You sure I can't interest you in a donation of mildewy paperbacks?"

"We're good, thank you." But he had a twinkle in his eye as he said it.

Lord, I've spent the whole day looking at dusty old newspaper archives, and I'm no closer to knowing the answer than when I started. Help me solve this problem for Tabitha, and for Trent and Tiffy.

CHAPTER NINE

"Hi, Logan. How was your day?" Tabitha asked as he slipped in the kitchen door to avoid the guests lounging in the library.

She was preparing dinner, which looked to be yet another almost-gourmet meal created from a range of fresh ingredients. Her ability to produce something from almost nothing was near magical after years of mass-produced boarding school, college dorm, and youth hostel meals.

Logan swallowed. "Moderately successful. The physical therapist is pleased with my progress and says I'm well enough to go ahead with being a camp counselor."

"That's great news." Tabitha's flat tone suggested it wasn't, which didn't make sense. Surely she didn't want him to stay?

"I visited the library as well. Mr. Masters sends his regards. He says he misses his chats with Martha."

"Gran was a great reader—which you know, because you've seen her bookshelves. She spent a lot of time at the library." Tabitha offered him a tight-lipped smile, a smile that suggested she was struggling to hold back tears. "Did you find any articles or photographs to support the lakefront zoning?"

"Nothing. I started in 1954 and worked backwards. Didn't find anything that implied the lake had ever flooded, certainly not high enough to affect the boat shed."

"So what do we do next?" Tabitha turned back toward the stove.

"I think it's time to get a professional opinion." Logan pulled out his phone and tapped on the screen. "I've found a surveyor and an engineer who've both done previous work in this area, and who should be able to provide a report that's robust enough to take to whichever committee is in charge of zoning applications. Take a look."

Logan pushed the phone across the kitchen counter toward Tabitha.

"How much is this going to cost?" She moved to the sink to wash her hands.

"It doesn't typically cost anything to get a quote. I suggest getting two or three quotes and see what they say—what they'll cover, how much they'll charge, and how quickly they can get the work done."

Tabitha dried her hands, then tapped the phone. "Is this the surveyor you're suggesting we contact?"

"Scroll right, and you'll see the others I've found," Logan said.

Tabitha scrolled right and left and left again. "They all seem like professionals who know what they're talking about. I'll ask Dad what he thinks when he gets home. He called to say he'd be working late tonight."

"Isn't it book club tonight?" Logan asked.

"Book club is on Thursday."

"Today is Thursday."

The third Thursday in March, which she'd said was book club night. Was Tabby so busy that she'd lost track of the day of the week? She needed a break.

Lord, You know Tabitha's heart. You know she wants to love You and serve You. But I'm worried that she's too busy working for You, that she's not spending time with You, not listening to You. I know that's not my place to say, as it's something I've done often enough, but I'm worried she's focusing on her grandmother's dream instead of her own calling.

"Already? Then yes, book club is tonight." She sighed, picked up the knife, and continued chopping vegetables. "I'll have to cancel. Tonight's guests aren't due to check in until eight, and I don't think Dad will be home in time. I'll be glad when tax time is over."

"Have you read the book?"

"Yes."

"Then you go to book club. I can check the guests in." He'd rather spend the evening with Tabitha, but she needed a break. He could email some people he knew and ask for recommendations on who they could approach to check out the boat shed.

"Are you sure? Do you know how?"

"They'll be going in the front suite, right? The one we cleaned this morning?"

"That's right." She added the vegetables to the casserole dish on the stovetop, put the lid on, and adjusted the temperature.

"I give them the key and show them the dining room. Anything else?"

"Find out what time they want breakfast." She pulled a package of what looked like chicken breast from the fridge and placed it on the counter. "Can you pass me the flour from the pantry?"

"That's anytime between seven and nine, right?" Logan extracted the flour tin and closed the pantry door.

"Yes—ask them what time they'd prefer and write it on the blackboard." She gestured toward the rustic blackboard hanging on the fridge door.

"Anything else? Do I need to take a payment? I don't know how to do that."

"No need. They booked through one of those last-minute booking sites, so they've already paid." She placed a frying pan on the stove, turned on the element, and drizzled oil into the pan.

"I didn't realize you listed with online sites."

"I list last-minute vacancies on one of the sites. They take a percentage, but it's more money than the room going vacant." She sounded flustered, as though she was thinking about something else as she answered his questions. Dinner, perhaps.

"So all I need to do is give them the key and the grand tour. I can do that." He injected a tone of bright confidence into his words. Maybe that would reassure her.

"Could you? I would be grateful." Was that relief he heard in her voice?

"It's no problem. Anytime. You need to get out more." Out with him would be better . . . if he ever summoned up courage to ask her out. In the meantime, he'd take what he could get. "You go to book club and enjoy yourself. I'll keep watch here."

Tabitha thanked him with a genuine smile this time as she placed the chicken in the pan to fry, a smile that filled the secret places in his heart he'd not known he wanted to fill.

CHAPTER TEN

The next day, Tabby made a point of arriving at work a few minutes early. She'd enjoyed book club the previous evening. Logan had been right—she'd needed to get away from the inn and spend time with her friends. She knocked on Hannah's open door.

"Do you have a few minutes?" Tabby asked.

"I have a tour group arriving in ten minutes, but I'm free until they arrive." Hannah shifted a pile of papers off the other chair, then sat back behind her overflowing desk.

"Logan has been doing some research on floodplains. He went to the library—"

"The library? I wouldn't expect them to have much information on floodplains."

"He was looking through the newspaper archive. He also checked the council records, and he's been searching online."

"Online? Is he using reputable websites? You know half of what's on the internet is wrong, and most of the rest is inaccurate."

Thank you, Hannah. Just because Tabby hadn't gone to some fancy Eastern college didn't mean she couldn't spot a dodgy website. "He's been reading sites like FEMA. It seems there are a lot of federal guidelines and information about floodplains."

"Like what?"

"Like how land is designated as a floodplain. Hannah, something's wrong. The lakefront doesn't meet any of the guidelines."

"There must be some reason why it's zoned as a floodplain. The default would be residential or commercial."

"That's what Logan said. We figured maybe there was a big flood or something."

"I don't remember any big floods. Or any stories of big floods."

"That's why Logan went to the library." Tabby slumped back in the chair. "We figured a flood would be news—enough to make the *Trinity Gazette*, at least."

"What did he find?" Hannah sounded intrigued.

"Nothing. Absolutely nothing."

"So how and why was the land zoned as a floodplain if there's no record of any floods?" Hannah switched hands and kept twirling the pen.

"Exactly. Logan says there are scientific studies you can do that prove whether land is a floodplain or not."

"How would he know?" Hannah's tone had turned disbelieving. "Wait. That sounded rude—"

"I know what you mean. He's an outdoor, sporty kind of guy, not a pencil-pushing, obey-the-rules kind of guy." Although he must have pushed a few pencils to graduate college.

"Yeah."

"He says his degree was in geography. And his dad works for a firm that manages construction projects. He's worked all over the world, including here in the States."

"So these scientific studies . . ."

"Logan says we can hire an engineer to investigate and give us a view on whether the land is a floodplain or not."

"And if it's not?"

"Then I guess we'd be able to petition the council to get the zoning changed."

Hannah tapped her forefinger against her chin. "If your land isn't actually a floodplain . . . what impact would that have on my land?"

"I guess you'd be able to petition the council for a zoning change as well."

"That's what I was thinking. I can't imagine that my land would be a floodplain and yours wouldn't. Or vice versa."

"I agree. Logan says—"

"Logan says a lot. You two seem to be spending a lot of time together." Hannah raised her eyebrows and winked.

"He's staying at the inn. Of course we're spending time together." Tabby forced an innocent tone into her words.

"Are you sure that's all?" Hannah knew her too well.

"That's all. Anyway, I'm surprised you've noticed, given the amount of time you're spending with your Australian tiler, and the amount of time he spends here. Anything you want to tell me?"

"We're training together. That's all. Anyway, we were talking about Logan, not Joel."

Hannah was talking about Logan. Tabby was trying to not talk about Logan.

Hannah had her thinking face on again, eyes crinkled in concentration, and fingers tapping against her lips. "Logan . . . I knew the name rang a bell, back when he first arrived, and I've finally worked it out. Isn't Logan Mr. Almost Perfect, the guy you described as Henry Cavill meets Heath Ledger? The guy you could barely breathe around, let alone talk to?"

She'd told Hannah that?

"He is. I can see it on your face." Hannah sat forward, looking like the cat who'd found the milk, the cream, and the entire cow. "Oh, this is getting interesting."

Interesting for Hannah. Less interesting for Tabby. More like a conversation she wanted to get out of as fast as possible.

"So Logan is the guy you've had a crush on for years, and he's staying with you and you're spending a lot of time together . . ."

Where was Hannah going with this, and where were the annoying club members and customers when she needed them?

"So you're either going to be completely cured of your crush, or you're going to fall head over heels in love with the guy." Hannah sounded triumphant. "I'd bet on the head over heels."

A buzzer sounded, indicating someone—or someones—had entered the building.

"That sounds like your tour group. I'll go and check them in." Saved by the buzzer.

"You do that. But don't think this conversation is over." Hannah shook her head with a I'm-not-going-to-forget-this smirk.

———

LOGAN WANDERED off the veranda and across to the boathouse. Tabby's dream had captured his attention, his imagination, his sense of obligation. And his desire to pay the Thomas family back for being his surrogate family over the years.

Lord, I feel You reminding me to trust You, that You will show me the path I'm meant to take, but I don't see any path ahead of me. Is this You saying I'm not trusting, that I'm falling back into my old patterns of leaning on my own understanding? I think it is. Lord, help me to trust You and to leave my future in Your hands.

He wouldn't try and go inside the boat shed. But he could look around outside.

The front quarter of the building projected out over the water, as Tabby had said. He walked along the lakeshore to see if he could get a better view of the front of the building. About half a kilometer from the building, the lakeshore curved enough that he could look back.

A roller door the width of the building faced the lake. If he was managing this renovation project, he'd replace that with bifold glass doors to bring in the sunlight, and so the customers could appreciate the view. Perhaps they could even add a front veranda to improve the indoor-outdoor flow . . . or would they need council consent to extend further into the lake? That might depend on the state of the building and whether there was a veranda on the original plans.

He walked back toward the boat shed, mentally calculating the size and the number of windows he'd recommend along each side. No, perhaps he'd only put windows on one side. East or west? West, to catch the afternoon sun and Trinity's golden sunsets. That would appeal to wedding planners or people looking for a venue for a classy afternoon tea or romantic evening meal. Although east-facing windows would allow the sun to heat the building during the day . . .

He wiped one of the grimy windows with his sleeve and peered inside. There was more grime on the inside of the window than the outside, if such a thing was possible. As such, he couldn't see much, just a pile of detritus to his left, covering what looked like wooden floors. Hopefully they'd be in good enough condition to keep. Polished wood floors would be easy to clean and maintain and would add to the venue's character.

Goodness. He was thinking and planning as if renovating and refurbishing the boat shed into a wedding venue or café or something was an absolute certainty, not a mere possibility.

He continued around the building. It looked like there was water and electricity at the south end. He'd recommend putting the entrance and guest bathrooms there, backing onto the kitchen. That would give them easy access to the road for deliveries.

But they had a lot of work ahead of them. Even the outside

stank worse than a football locker room. Tabby had said she thought birds lived underneath and inside, and it certainly smelled like it, even from out here.

Thinking of underneath . . . what were the foundations like? He wasn't going into the water to find out. Inspecting piles and foundations was a job best left to the professionals.

Logan walked around the outside of the building again, this time paying particular attention to the condition of the weatherboards, to see if he could estimate how much work needed to be done. He was no contractor, but he'd spent enough time around building and renovation projects to have picked up the basics.

Surprisingly little work needed doing, as it turned out. Despite what Tabby had said about the boat shed being abandoned for twenty-odd years, it wasn't uncared for. There was clear evidence it had undergone major repairs sometime this century, with more recent minor upkeep as well.

He walked around the other side of the boat shed, the side facing away from Trinity Lakes and the Lakeview Inn. These boards were obviously new—the paint was smoother, and none of it was peeling off, despite getting the full afternoon sun.

He looked again. Some of the boards on the town side were slightly out, as though they weren't in their original positions. He walked around again. Yes, he was right. Whoever had repaired the building had replaced the rotting boards on the town side with boards from the far side, then used new boards on the far side . . . where the work wouldn't be noticed, perhaps so the work—or the worker—wouldn't be seen.

But who had performed the work? And who had paid for it?

CHAPTER ELEVEN

By Easter, Tabby and Logan had finished clearing out Gran's bedroom and bathroom. Tabby organized for Joel to visit and quote for retiling the bathroom, and Logan arranged for Jasper Cohen to quote on repainting the bedroom. Both delivered their quotations promptly, but both had full schedules and wouldn't be able to start work until after Memorial Day.

It was a pity the room wouldn't be finished any earlier, but Tabby had only herself to blame for not getting organized. And if it wasn't for Logan's help, the room would still be a mess. Logan had also organized quotes for the boat shed, one from a surveyor in Seattle, and the other from an engineer in Walla Walla.

Now it was time to talk to Dad. Tabby gathered the printed quotes and found him settling down with a book in the family lounge.

"Do you have a moment?" She offered him the papers.

"Sure." Dad put his book down and took the small pile of papers. "What am I looking at?"

"Quotes for renovating Gran's bathroom and painting her bedroom," Tabby said as Logan walked in.

"You're getting Cohens to do the work?"

"The bedroom, yes. Justin and Joel are going to do the bathroom, just the same as they've done the other three."

"Then go ahead and do it. You don't need me." He thrust the papers back to Tabby, but she didn't take them.

"There's also quotes to survey the boat shed. To prove it's not a floodplain."

"Why?"

"To get the council to rezone the lakefront land, so we can renovate the boat shed."

Dad flicked between the two quotes, comparing what each quote promised, and the prices.

"The engineer is more expensive, but she's local, has a good reputation, and the city has used her before. They're less likely to argue with someone they trust," Logan said.

"Have you talked to Tiffy and Trent about any of this?" Dad asked.

"Not yet. I wanted to have something to tell them first."

"Then it's time to bring them up to speed and make sure they're on board with whatever you're planning on doing and spending."

"But you make all the decisions. You always have."

"You're all adults. It's time you three started making the decisions. Give Tiffy and Trent a call." Dad picked up his book and left the room.

Tabby checked her phone. Trent would be home from work, and Tiffy would probably be studying. Tiffy was always studying.

She pulled up their sibling chat and hit the video call button. Both answered almost immediately—unusual.

"Hi, Trent. Hi, Tiffy," Tabby said. "We need to have a family meeting."

"What's up?" Trent asked. "We're not the 'family meeting' kind of family."

"Can we make this quick?" Tiffy asked. "Finals start soon, and you have no idea how much studying I have to do."

"Logan and I—"

"Logan? Logan's still with you?" Tiffy asked.

"Logan's staying here until camp starts."

Logan moved behind Tabby so he could be seen on the screen and waved to Tiffy and Trent. "I've been helping out around the place and doing some research for Tabby."

For which Tabby was grateful. She hadn't realized how many little things Gran had taken care of, even when she was ill.

All things that Tabby needed to take care of now.

"Hey, Logan." Trent waved.

"Hi, Logan. Nice to see you and all, but I don't have time for idle chit-chat, so can we please cut to the chase? Like I said, I should be studying." Tiffany sounded more stressed than usual.

"Logan and I were cleaning out Gran's room and we found the deed to the boat shed."

"The boat shed? The one across the road?" Tiffy twirled a pen.

"Why would Gran have had the deed?" Trent asked. "I remember her telling me the family used to own all that lakefront land. Grandpa had thought about putting cabins along the lakefront, but there was some reason he couldn't, so he sold the land."

"He used to own it all?" That was news to Tabby.

"You should be able to check down at city hall, but I'm sure that's what she told me." Trent's tone was serious.

"Did your grandmother say anything about the zoning along the lakefront?" Logan angled the computer toward himself.

"Nope."

"Yes," Tiffy said. "I remember her talking about the view from the front veranda. I said it would be horrible if someone built something big and ugly right in front of us, and she said they couldn't because of the land zone. I think that was about the same time as Mr. Gilbertson bought the rowing club."

"Did she mention anything about flooding or a floodplain?" Tabby asked.

"No," Tiffy said.

"Not that I heard," Trent said. "Why?"

"All the lakefront land, from the boat shed to the rowing club, is a designated floodplain, which means the council won't allow anything to be built there."

"You mentioned the boat shed. Why?" Trent asked.

"Apparently we own the boat shed as well as the inn," Tabby said.

"We?" Tiffy frowned.

"We. The three of us." Tabby gestured to the faces on the computer screen.

"We own the boat shed and the inn?" Trent had the same slightly confused look Tabby must have had when she first learned the truth.

"Can we sell the boat shed?" Typical Tiffany. It always came back to money. Mind you, if Tabby had Tiffy's student loans—and another two or three years before she finished med school—perhaps she'd be more obsessed with money.

"Is the boat shed worth selling?" Trent, as usual, got to the heart of the matter.

"What's the zoning got to do with the boat shed?" Tiffy asked.

"The zoning is relevant because it will affect the value of the land," Logan said. "You need special permits and insurance to build on a floodplain, and that's going to affect the market value."

"Won't you also need permits for upgrading an existing property on a floodplain?" Trent asked.

"Correct," Logan said.

"So the run-down boat shed Dad told us we were never to go in, on pain of death or worse . . . we own it?" Tiffy did not sound pleased. "But we can't do any work on it without some special permit, which means we probably can't sell it either? Great."

"But why are you telling us this?" Trent asked. "The boat shed has been sitting there for decades, getting more and more run-down. It can stay rotting for another few decades. Unless the council has decided it's some kind of health and safety hazard."

This time Tiffy did roll her eyes. "It's been a health and safety hazard our entire lives."

"It's actually had some work done," Logan said.

"What kind of work?"

"Since when?" Tabby asked at the same time.

"Recently—possibly in the last few months. Certainly in the last year. There's a brand-new padlock on the front door." Logan flicked through the papers on the kitchen counter, withdrew the boat shed blueprint, and held it up to the camera. "There are new boards around the back, where we can't see them. And it looks like some of the boards at the front—like here, here, and here . . ." He indicated the parts of the building closest to the road and to the inn. ". . . have had rotten boards replaced with old boards from around the west side."

"How can you tell?" Tabby asked.

"The paint is a slightly different shade of not-quite-white. It also looks like the back has been painted in the last few years."

"You mean someone has been replacing boards and painting the boat shed and we've never noticed?" Tabby couldn't believe what Logan was saying. He wouldn't be lying, but could someone really have repainted the boat shed without her noticing?

"How often does anyone ever look?" Trent leaned back in his chair and stretched. "I can't remember the last time I paid any attention to the boat shed."

"The exterior and roof look sound. But the interior is a mess —not that I could see much through the windows—and we'd need professionals to tell us if the foundations are solid."

We. Tabby liked the sound of "we."

"So what are you suggesting?" Tiffy folded her arms in front of the computer and leaned toward the screen.

"I want to hire an engineer to review the land and see if it really is a floodplain," Tabby said. "I wanted to let you know, as the co-owners."

"I've found a couple of people who could do the job." Logan tapped on the quotes sitting on the kitchen counter.

"What happens if the engineer says it's not a floodplain?" Tiffy picked up a pen. "Does that mean we can sell it?"

"Or fix it up ourselves. Gran wanted to turn it into an event venue. Her mother got married on the front veranda and had plans to restore it so other people could get married there."

"Competition with the country club?" Trent asked. "Sounds like a great idea."

"We could fix it up then sell it. That would make more money than selling it as it is." Tiffany spun a pen around her fingers.

"Or fix it up and keep it."

"And do what?"

"Turn it into a business," Tabby said. "Like Gran wanted."

"Who'd run it? Tiffy asked. "You have more than enough to do with the B&B." Tiffy understood all the work Tabby did around the place—cooking, cleaning, and keeping the public areas spotless.

"What do you know about running a business?" Trent might not have intended to sound condescending, but that was exactly how he sounded.

Tabby closed her eyes in a long, slow blink, and drew in a long, slow breath, praying for patience.

"Trent Allan Thomas. I've been running this business for the last four years. You might have the book learning, but I've got the practical experience."

Trent opened his mouth to reply, but Tabitha hadn't finished.

"Do you think I just make beds and cook breakfast?"

Trent nodded. Oh, this was going to be fun.

"Yes, I clean the rooms. I cook and serve breakfast. I clean the kitchen and the rest of the house. I also update the website, take the bookings, greet the guests, plan the menus, order the food, pay the bills, keep the accounts—"

"Doesn't Dad—" Trent gave Logan a "help me!" look, but Logan shook his head.

"I might not know how to develop a strategy or a business plan or any of that fancy theory you learned at college, but did you ever stop to think where all the money Dad gave you over the years came from? It came from here, from the inn, from me."

"Let's take one step at a time," Logan said. "There's no point debating who's going to do anything until you have a professional engineer's report and know if you can get the zoning changed."

"So get one." Tiffany's tone was decisive, but was that because she wanted to sell a property she'd only just found out she owned a one-third share in, or because she wanted to get back to her studies? This was Tiffy. It could be both.

"Trent? Do you agree?" Tabby asked.

"Depends." Trent drummed his fingers on the keyboard. "How much is this likely to cost? And how long will it take?"

"I'll email you the quotes. They said it would take around two weeks."

"Who is going to pay?" Tiffy twirled the pen again. "I don't have any money to spare."

"Dad says we can pay out of the inn's account," Tabby said. "I didn't want to do anything without you knowing. So is that okay?" They were triplets. They'd done everything together, good and bad, until Trent and Tiffy had gone off to college.

"Fine by me," Trent said.

"Fine by me, but do you really want to be a café owner or wedding coordinator as well as a B&B host?" Tiffy asked. "Don't you already have enough to do?"

"I want to do it in memory of Gran. It was her dream. She had a scrapbook full of ideas, complete with blueprints and quotes from Cohen's Hardware and the old Wainscott place."

"Wainscott Emporium? They went out of business while we were in grade school. I used to love going in there with Gran and look at the new stock while she ordered new sheets and towels for the inn." Tiffy leaned back and looked off camera, as though picturing the scene. "Anyway, gotta go. Call me back when you have news." Her camera clicked off, and black filled the screen before it switched back to Trent.

"Trent, you wanted to talk to Tabitha, didn't you?" Logan asked.

Tabby gave Logan a sideways look.

"I did?" Trent asked.

"You did." Logan gave Trent a narrow-eyed look and inclined his head toward Tabby.

"You think I need to talk to Tabby . . . why?"

"Oh, I don't know." She put on her best fake-innocent expression. "Maybe he thinks you should apologize to me for being a mansplaining boor, and that it's time to start groveling as a way of thanking me for financing your college education."

Logan gave a slow nod. "That about sums it up. I'm going to leave you two to your fun family conversation." He stood and headed toward the door, his limp almost gone. "Talk later, Trent."

"Later, Logan." Trent waved at Logan's back. "Sorry, Tabby. I thought Dad did the business stuff."

"Well, now you know. Gran passed all the banking to me

when she broke her leg and couldn't walk to the bank. In the second year, I did all the ordering and paid all the bills. In the third year, I started doing all the bookkeeping in the online program Dad set up. I do the same stuff here as I do for Hannah, except I do payroll for her as well."

"Sorry. I figured you just did the easy stuff. No. Wait. That sounds bad as well. I guess I figured Dad did the finances and you did the rest. Sorry. I should have paid attention and not assumed."

"You should have." But Trent had a long history of not paying attention to anything beyond himself. And he was her brother. "I forgive you."

"Changing the subject, how are you getting on with Logan? I feel a little guilty for dumping him on you, but he didn't have anywhere else to go."

"He's an excellent guest. He's been helping me clean out Gran's room, and he's done most of the research around the boat shed."

"Has he asked you out yet?"

And that was close to the last question she expected from Trent, who'd warned her about Logan before they'd even met.

"Why would he? He's not interested in me like that. Besides, I'd say no." He wasn't a Christian, even if he was pretty much the perfect guy in all other respects.

"It's no secret you've had a crush on him for years. He's a good guy. Why wouldn't you want to date him?"

And here she'd hoped her crush was her secret. "I wouldn't date him even if he asked. You warned me about him the first time we met. And you know I wouldn't date someone who wasn't a Christian."

"What do you mean?" Trent asked. "Of course he's a Christian."

What? Logan? A Christian? Surely not. Unless he'd recently

been saved. If so, glory, hallelujah, and praise the Lord. But . . .

"Since when?"

"Ever since I've known him." Trent gave her a how-can-you-not-know-this look.

"Logan is a Christian? Logan, the guy you introduced to me as 'wild Logan Wylde,' the guy who seemed to be sleeping off a party every time Tiffy went to visit you in your dorm?"

"I . . . um . . . I never knew that." Trent looked at the floor. She couldn't see his hands over the Zoom call, but she'd bet tomorrow's breakfast dishes that he was flicking his fingernails, his lifetime guilty tell.

"Tiffy said there were times when your dorm room had more empty bottles than the campus bar. You weren't old enough to drink, so they must have been Logan's." Although Logan was only two years older, so even he hadn't been of legal drinking age back then.

Trent didn't look up.

"They were Logan's, right?"

Silence.

"They were your empty bottles? You were drinking? And drinking a lot, based on what Tiffy said." Tabby folded her arms and gave Trent her best oldest-sister death stare. So what if she was only older by thirty minutes.

"Everyone was drinking," Trent said. "Well, almost everyone. Not Tiffy. She was always studying." So Trent had been drinking—and to excess, if Tiffy was right. And Tiffy was usually right.

"What about Logan?" Not that Logan drinking or not drinking made Logan a Christian or not a Christian. She knew Christians who drank as well as non-Christians who didn't. But if Logan didn't drink and he wasn't the party animal . . .

"Logan didn't usually drink. He always used early-morning training as an excuse. If we were going somewhere off campus, he'd volunteer to be the designated driver." So Trent hadn't been drinking and driving. That was a relief.

"That wasn't what we're talking about." She sat back and folded her arms across her chest. "We're talking about whether Logan is a Christian or not."

"He is. Ask him."

"If Logan is a Christian, why did you warn me away from him?"

"He was heading for the big league—the NFL. Endless training camps and traveling the country for months at a time. There's no way Dad would have let you travel with him even if you'd wanted to, but you also wouldn't have wanted a long-distance relationship."

Trent wasn't wrong. She'd tried the long-distance thing once, with her high school boyfriend. It had ended when he'd broken up with her by text the week before Thanksgiving, the same Thanksgiving she'd first met Logan. He-who-they-did-not-name then had the gall to turn up in Trinity Lakes for Thanksgiving with a new girlfriend in tow.

"And after that? After he lost his place in the NFL?"

"He went through a bad patch. Didn't know what to do with his life. That's not a recipe for a lasting relationship."

Hope flickered in Tabby's chest. "I asked him if he wanted to come to church with me on Sunday afternoon, and he turned me down flat."

"Isn't the evening service a repeat of the morning service? Maybe he'd already been."

So many people worked in tourism in Trinity Lakes that they'd been repeating the morning service in the evening for as long as Tabby could remember. On that basis, it was more than possible Logan had been to the morning service. He'd disappeared after helping her clean the guest rooms, and she hadn't asked where he'd gone.

And Trinity Lakes had so many tourists that a single guy

turning up to church once wouldn't be remarked on—everyone would assume he was a weekend visitor. The Rhondas didn't go full matchmaker until they'd seen the same single guy in church at least twice.

Logan usually volunteered to clear up after breakfast so she could start on the rooms. He'd put the laundry on for her, then disappear, just like he did weekdays when they weren't clearing out Gran's room. She'd never asked where he was going—that was his own private business—but she'd assumed he'd headed to the gym.

Had he been going to church? Maybe she could ask. Because if Logan was a Christian . . . that raised some interesting possibilities.

CHAPTER TWELVE

A week had passed since the family Zoom call. A week in which Tabby had mentally reviewed every interaction between her and Logan in the five weeks since he'd arrived and prayed more than she'd prayed since Gran died.

And she'd come to a few conclusions.

First, she wished she could talk this all over with Gran. Gran had always been her counselor and confidant, discussing matters of faith and matters of the heart as they cooked and cleaned.

Sure, Dad was great, and he did his best to always be there for her, but there were some subjects she wanted a woman's view on. Logan was one of those subjects.

Second, Logan was a great guy, and it was okay to be attracted to him. More than okay. He was a Christian. He was kind and gentle and a hard worker. Some people might judge him for having a bunch of dead-end jobs rather than pursuing some fancy high-paid career, but those people would say the same about her.

Finally, and perhaps more importantly, he appeared to like

her as well, if their conversations in Gran's room and on the veranda were any indication.

But she'd actively been brushing him off for the last however long. Weeks? Certainly. Months? Probably. Years. Possibly.

Now she needed to cast off the habit of years long gone and allow her interest to show. Just in case it was reciprocated. And she hoped it was.

A verse came to mind, reminding her that God was not slow in keeping His promises. *God, if it's all the same to You, if Logan's interested in me, then I'd rather know sooner than later. Like, lots sooner.*

If she remembered correctly, the verse was about people coming to repentance and belief in God, not people coming to the realization that someone else had already come to repentance and belief in God.

Another verse came to mind, about forgiving others. Like Trent.

She had to forgive Trent for his lies, the lies that had potentially kept her and Logan apart. But if the Bible was right about God doing everything in His appointed time, then this must be the appointed time.

No one was checking out of the inn today, which meant she had a couple of hours free once she'd served breakfast and freshened the guest rooms. She had a plan, a surprise for Logan.

First, breakfast.

Logan took his usual seat in the dining room.

"Good morning, Logan. Do you have any plans for today?" Tabitha set his plate in front of him.

"Nothing in particular. Why do you ask?"

"Because I was going through Gran's desk again, and I found a key." She produced an almost-new key from her pocket, the kind of key that looked as though it could fit any modern door —or padlock—and held it up in front of her.

"A key for what?"

"Guess."

"A castle. A dragon's lair. The cupboard under the stairs."

"We don't have a cupboard under the stairs." Tabitha gave an exaggerated roll of her eyes.

"Then . . . a mysterious attic?"

Tabitha shook her head. "The boat shed."

"The boat shed? How do you know?"

"Because Gran, who couldn't organize a receipt or an invoice to save herself, managed to put the key in an envelope and label the envelope." She held out the key. "Didn't you tell Trent there's a new-looking padlock on the boat shed door?"

"I did." Logan took the key and rolled it around in his fingers. "Let's sort out the guests and explore the boat shed."

Two hours later, after the chores were done, they headed over to the boat shed, unlocked the padlock, and opened the door.

Tabby moved carefully into the building, picking her way through detritus and debris to the center of the large room, then turned in a slow circle to take in the space. She closed her eyes and turned again, imagining what Gran had pictured in her scrapbook, imagining what the room could be.

"What do you see?" Logan asked.

"Right now?" Tabby stopped turning. "I see work. A lot of work. But I also see what it could become." A café. A restaurant. An event venue. Gran's dream.

"And what's that?"

"A wedding venue. Perhaps a café or restaurant that could also do weddings." She hadn't been the kind of girl who'd spent years planning her dream wedding before she'd even had her first kiss. But she loved occasions, and she loved cooking. What better combination than cooking for weddings and other occasions?

"What work would you want done?" Logan moved around the inside, hands in pockets as if taking stock.

"I'd keep the open beams." She pointed above their heads. "I've seen pictures of places with nautical pieces hanging from the roof. Fishing nets, lobster pots, even a rowboat."

"There's a café back home like that. A nautical theme. Trinity is a lake, so perhaps fishing rods and floats rather than lobster pots. What else?"

"Wooden walls with local fishing photos and memorabilia." A hodgepodge of pictures in unmatched frames, a contrast to the artwork featured on the inn's whitewashed walls.

"Nice. Where would you get them?"

"Gran's room. Our attic. The library. There's probably stuff in here we could use."

"The library's newspaper archive might have some pictures you could use."

"Good idea. I'd like lots of old pictures in antique-looking frames."

There were stacks of debris and junk in the far corner. Trash, or might there be something useful?

"What's over there?" Tabby asked.

"Looks like rubbish."

She moved toward the pile of debris, then prodded it with a foot to see if there was anything useful. Something shiny caught her eye, so she stretched her foot a little further and lost her balance.

Logan caught her from behind, and pulled her into his arms, turning her so they were face to face, holding her tightly enough to prevent her falling but not so tightly that she couldn't step away.

She didn't step away.

"Careful." His smile was hot enough to melt glass. "You said this place might be dangerous."

"Maybe I was right." Because this hold, this embrace, felt dangerous.

Logan rested his hands on her hips and leaned close, but not the kind of close that suggested he was leaning in to tell a joke or share a secret. More the kind of close that suggested he was about to kiss her . . . assuming those Hallmark movies she'd watched with Hannah and Leah were even halfway right.

Her sensible, responsible side wanted to step backward, out of his arms, out of his encompassing embrace.

Her undeveloped, underutilized adventurous side, the side she'd stifled for so long, wanted to lean in, to press herself against him, to be one with him.

"Can I kiss you?" he whispered—no, breathed—against her lips.

So those Hallmark movies were right. He had moved in for a kiss. Their first kiss.

What was the right response? It probably wasn't debating the question, whether the question should have been "Can I" or "May I." And the correct answer probably wasn't "Yes, please."

"Tabitha? Can I kiss you?"

"Yes. Kiss me." Please. Before she ruined the moment by saying something stupid. Like "please."

His lips touched hers, feather light and warm and . . . and oh my goodness. The Hallmark Channel hadn't been lying.

She wrapped her arms around his neck as he put his arms around her waist and his lips moved against hers. A thrill shot through her core. If this was kissing, she now knew why it had inspired untold songs and stories, novels and movies.

It was breathtaking.

Spellbinding.

Magic.

Like fireworks and fantasies and a future.

And she didn't want it to end.

Logan ended the kiss and rested his forehead against hers. "Wow."

"Wow, indeed." It had been more years than she cared to count since she'd kissed a guy, and now she had to act like the mature adult she pretended to be and not beg for another kiss or three.

"I could keep kissing you all morning, but you probably need to get to work sometime today."

"I do. But I want to finish checking out the possibilities in here first." She meant the building but was open to being misinterpreted.

"So you can see open beams, wood-paneled walls, and a nautical theme." Logan turned her and held her from behind. "What else?"

"Wooden floors. More windows." More kissing?

"What do you think of bifold glass doors opening onto a veranda, looking out over the lake? And an outdoor seating area?" Logan indicated the wooden roller doors at the front of the building which opened out onto the lake.

"I like that idea. Especially the veranda." She stepped out of his hold and turned to look down the length of the building. "The view is here, so the kitchen will need to be at the back."

"Makes sense." Logan reached for her hand, rubbing her knuckles as they ambled to the back of the building, to where the kitchen would have to go.

"Bathrooms by the entrance, and kitchen on the other side." Tabby gestured left and right with her free hand, the hand that wasn't tingling from his touch.

"What would you want in the kitchen?" He looked at her with a half-smile, suggesting he knew that she knew exactly what she wanted.

"A proper commercial kitchen—stainless steel countertops and gas burners and a walk-in refrigerator and commercial dishwashers and sterilizers."

"What else?" Logan released her hand and dropped another quick kiss. Just one. One was not enough.

"Storage." She turned slowly, picturing where she'd position each item, wishing he'd hold her hand again.

"What kind of storage?"

"Tables, chairs, decorations. So we could use the space for different kinds of events."

"You're thinking of an event venue rather than a café?"

"I don't think Trinity Lakes has the population to support another café or restaurant. Catering for events would give more flexibility than a café." Managing and catering events would mean she didn't have to be tied down to working every day, like she was with the inn.

"You could target tourists for a café or restaurant. They'd want the waterfront view."

"So would brides and birthday girls." She closed her eyes and pictured the lake as a backdrop to wedding photographs. It would be gorgeous.

"So you want to do weddings."

Weddings. Romance. Kissing. No. She needed to concentrate. Pretend she was a competent and professional woman talking about her future business. Here. In the boat shed.

"And anniversaries. Birthday parties. Mother's Day. Maybe even small business functions." That's right. Something that wasn't romantic. Think, Tabby. She forced her mind back to the boat shed, to Gran's dream. Would she be able to cook for a crowd? Cook more than the seven breakfasts on the inn's menu since she was a teenager? Deliver food on a schedule?

"Who's going to run it?" Was his tone a little too casual?

"You don't think I could run a restaurant or organize a wedding?" She couldn't hide the hurt.

"You?" He slung an arm around her shoulder and pulled her towards him. "Tabitha, you could organize a fancy shindig with one hand tied behind your back. Well, perhaps not literally, but yeah, you could do it."

"So why ask?" She turned back to face him and put her hands around his waist, and he pulled her close.

"Because you've already got enough on your plate. You've

got a full-time job at the rowing club, and running the inn is basically another full-time job. Running a restaurant or event business as well? That's . . ."

Crazy. He didn't say it. He didn't have to. And maybe it was crazy, but that didn't mean she couldn't do it. Couldn't dream.

"And what about your pinboard full of postcards? Didn't you want to travel?" Logan stepped back, dropping his hands to hold hers.

"Yeah . . ." She drew the word out. "But I also want to cook. I love feeding people."

"I've noticed." He offered a wry grin and swung their joined hands together. "You're always in the kitchen. So which would work better—café or restaurant or event venue?"

There were pluses and minuses either way. "Doing events might not earn as much as a restaurant but would give me more flexibility to take time off."

"That was what I was thinking. I guess we can work up business cases for both and see which has the most potential." He let go of one hand and turned towards the door.

Zoning, permits, business cases. Moving the junk, cleaning the space, washing the windows. There was a lot of work ahead.

But it was doable. Manageable. Achievable. Especially with Logan's help. Especially if she'd correctly interpreted the promise in that kiss.

She—they—could make Gran's dream come true.

———

"One, two, three, four." Tabby counted the cups of flour out loud so she didn't ruin the recipe by adding too few cups, or too many—both mistakes she'd made over the years when baking large batches. Both mistakes she was more likely to make when she was distracted . . . and distracted didn't even begin to describe how she felt this morning after yesterday's trip to the boatshed and last night's cuddling on the back veranda. She could barely breathe around Logan, let alone think.

"It's starting to feel like summer is on the way." Logan sat at the kitchen counter and took a mouthful of the ham and mushroom omelet she'd just made him. "We should take advantage of the weather and go out on the lake."

"Not today. I need to bake a batch of cookies for the young mother's group at church and I'm working at Hannah's at noon." She'd much rather spend time with Logan, but she'd promised Rhonda, and she refused to be one of those women who reneged on their responsibilities because of a man.

"I didn't say when."

"I figured you meant today."

"I was thinking of tomorrow. Saturday's your day off from the rowing club, isn't it?"

Was Logan suggesting a date?

"So let's go kayaking tomorrow. If it's not raining, of course."

"No, thank you." She'd love to go on a date with Logan, but kayaking? She'd rather clean Trent's bathroom with a toothbrush.

"You're always working. You need to give yourself a few hours off. Give yourself time to relax, to rest." *With me.* He didn't say the words, but she could hear them in his tone, see them in the way he looked at her. But kayaking?

"I don't kayak." Kayaking was scary and stressful, not relaxing or romantic.

"What about rowing or paddleboarding or sailing?"

"I don't row or paddleboard or sail either." She tried to modulate her tone to indicate she was interested in doing something social with Logan . . . as long as that something social had nothing to do with water.

"Do you waterski? Swim? You live beside a lake. You must do something aquatic."

"I can swim." She turned away from the kitchen island, back

to the sink. Did he have any suggestions that didn't involve water?

"If you don't kayak or paddleboard or row or sail, then it's time you learned."

"I didn't say I couldn't. I said I don't." Her heart beat faster at the thought.

"Why not?"

"I don't like the water. People drown."

"I'm a qualified lifeguard, a qualified first aider, a qualified sports and outdoors expert. There's nothing to be afraid of."

"It's not about being afraid. It's about being safe. Sensible. Having a healthy respect for water."

"I have a healthy respect for water. And I raft and kayak and swim." Logan crossed his arms across his chest. His broad, muscled chest.

Tabitha turned away and washed her hands. They didn't need washing, but she needed to not look at Logan. Otherwise, he'd convince her to do something stupid, like go kayaking on Lake Wainscott.

"Okay. You're not afraid of water. You have a 'healthy respect' for water. What happened to give you that healthy respect?"

Tabitha dried her hands on the kitchen towel, keeping her back to Logan.

"I could guess." Logan injected a hint of humor into his tone. "A crab bit you at the beach one summer, so now you don't like the water."

"It's a freshwater lake. There aren't any crabs." She turned around and leaned against the counter, unable to resist the temptation to watch him, watch his eyes twinkle, watch the way the right side of his mouth crept up as he tried to hold back a smile.

"Fair point. You used to be a champion swimmer in high

school but you gave it up to let someone else be champion so they could get a swimming scholarship and go to college."

"No."

"I know. You wore an itsy bitsy teeny weeny yellow polka dot bikini and had a wardrobe malfunction as you executed a perfect double somersault and half twist off the ten-meter platform, and that scarred you for life."

"Now you're being silly."

"A handful of humor helps the hurt go down." He leaned forward, elbows on the counter, and rested his chin in his hands. "What's the real problem? Is it that you don't want to go kayaking? Or that you don't want to go with me?"

"It's not you. It's me." She slapped her hand over her mouth. "Oh, that sounded awful. It really isn't you. It's me. And water. I . . . I just don't do water."

"You live beside a lake. You work at a rowing club. But you don't do water. Did something happen? When you were younger?"

She was silent.

Was he going to keep asking until she told him why?

Probably.

Should she tell him?

Probably.

Sure. She and Tiffy and Trent had sworn that long-ago pinkie promise not to tell. But that was sixteen years ago. A lifetime ago. And her childish decision had almost cost a life.

She stared blankly ahead, her mouth set in a firm line.

"What happened? You don't have to tell me. But it might help."

She leaned back against the counter and wrapped her arms around her middle.

"It was the summer we were seven. There are always fireworks over the lake on the night of the Fourth of July. Gran said we'd have to take an afternoon nap if we wanted to stay up and watch the fireworks."

"Let me guess. You were too old for a nap."

"We thought we were. Tiffany would have been happy lying in bed and reading a book, but Trent . . ."

"Trent has never been one to sit still."

"So I suggested we all go down to the lake." When she closed her eyes, it was as though she were seven years old again.

Gran never let them go to the lake on their own. Gran said they were too little. Gran didn't understand. They had finished first grade. They were big now. So they'd snuck out and crossed the road to the lakefront park. The park was empty except for two big, black trucks.

"Trent, what do the words on the truck say?" Tiffy asked.

Trent was better at reading than Tabby or Tiffy. He was the clever one. That was what Daddy always said. His voice would go all funny when he said it. "Trent, you're a chip off the old block," he'd say.

"Py-ro-tech-nic. Pyrotechnic. Powers Pyrotechnics," Trent said.

"What does that mean?" Tabby asked.

Tiffy knew. "It must be the fireworks people." She pointed toward the middle of the lake, where workers in black uniforms with red and yellow flames were working on barges.

Trent wandered around the back of the truck, and Tiffy followed.

"I wonder what fireworks look like before they're set off," Tiffy said. Daddy never bought fireworks for the Fourth of July. He said they didn't need them, because Trinity Lakes had the best display in Washington.

"Let's kayak out to the barges and have a look," Trent said. The inn had two kayaks for guests to use, and they were kept in the old boat shed.

"What about lifejackets?" Tabby asked. The lifejackets weren't kept in the boat shed—they were kept in the house.

"We don't need lifejackets," Trent said. "We all passed our swimming tests at school."

Tabby gave Tiffy an "are you sure" look. Trent didn't know, but Tiffy hadn't passed the test. She'd been awarded the certificate, but only because Tabby had taken the test twice rather than let Tiffy fail.

Tiffy nodded. "We'll be all right. We're not going to fall out."

They pulled the larger kayak to the lake and climbed in. Tabby sat in the front, Trent in the back, and Tiffy in the middle. Trent pushed off. Tabby set the pace and Tiffy matched her, as they always had. But Trent was used to being the one in charge, even though he was the youngest, and even though he was seated at the back.

They were halfway between the lakeshore and the barge when Tiffy shouted that she'd lost her paddle. Tabby tried to backpaddle to get in position to retrieve it, Tiffy leaned left to grab the paddle, leaned too far, and fell out with a huge splash.

"Here! Grab this!" Trent shouted.

Tabby turned to see Trent holding his paddle out toward Tiffy, but she bobbed under the water, arms flailing as she struggled to stay afloat, already too panicked to reach for Trent's paddle.

Trent leaned out a little further.

And dropped the paddle.

"Why is she sinking?" Trent asked.

"Because she can't swim, stupid."

"I'm going to dive in." The kayak rocked as Trent moved behind her.

"Stop! You're rocking the kayak. I'll fall out, and the kayak will float away, and we'll have nothing to hold onto."

"What are we going to do?"

"Lean over and catch her as she comes up for air."

It was a good plan. For a seven-year-old.

But Tiffy didn't come up for air.

"Hey! You two!" A voice came from the shore—the Junk Man. That wasn't his real name, but no one ever called him by his real name. Tabby didn't even know what his real name was.

"What's the matter?" he shouted.

"It's Tiffy," Tabby called back. "She's fallen into the lake."

"Don't shout," Trent said. "If Dad or Gran hears, we're going to be in so much trouble."

They'd be in more trouble if they couldn't save Tiffy.

Panic crawled from her stomach up to her mouth. She couldn't talk, couldn't think, couldn't breathe. Her sister, her twin sister, was in the water, under the water, and Tiffy couldn't swim. Couldn't save herself.

"You stay there," the Junk Man called. "I'll find her." He waded into the water in all his clothes and swam toward them. "Where did she go down?" the Junk Man asked as he got closer.

"There." Tabby indicated toward the left. "By the paddle."

The Junk Man duck-dived down, moving under the water with a grace he'd never shown on land. Down, up, down, up.

"She's down here." Under he went again and came up holding a sodden Tiffy. He hefted her over his shoulder and thumped her on the back like she was an oversized baby who needed to burp.

Would she be okay? Was she breathing? Was she even alive?

"Follow me." The Junk Man headed to shore.

Tabby dug deep and paddled toward shore.

Please, God, let Tiffy be alive. Let her be all right.

"Wait. You need to get the paddles," Trent said. "Otherwise Dad will find out."

Tabby didn't have the energy to answer. Of course Dad was going to find out. So was Gran. The Junk Man would tell them for sure.

She was the oldest. This was all her fault. Dad was going to be so angry. And was Tiffy going to be okay? She dug harder with her paddle, pushing to get back to Tiffy faster.

By the time they got to shore, the Junk Man had Tiffy lying on her side on the grass. She'd vomited and was coughing like she was going to vomit again. But she was alive. She was breathing. She was going to be okay. Tabby didn't know how she knew, but she did. The thing clawing inside her chest disappeared and she could breathe again. Think again. Live again.

Thank You, God.

"Are you all right?" Tabby patted her on the back the way Gran did when they were sick.

"Am. Now." Tiffy coughed again.

Tabby turned to the Junk Man. "You saved her life. Thank you so much." There was no way she—they—could ever repay this strange man.

"What were you three doing out on the lake anyway?" the Junk Man asked. His voice was gruff and rough and rusty, as though he hadn't spoken in a while. "Without supervision and without lifejackets?"

"We wanted to see the fireworks," Tabby said.

"Please don't tell anyone," Trent said.

"I won't," the Junk Man said. "But you have to promise me never to go into the lake again without an adult."

"Pinkie promise?" Tiffy asked.

"Pinkie promise." And the Junk Man had held out his pinkie finger just like she and Tiffy did, and they'd pinkie promised never to tell, and never to go on the lake again.

"Then the Junk Man told us to get inside, that he'd find the missing paddles and put the kayak away. We managed to get inside without Gran or Dad finding us. We got Tiffany changed into dry clothes and spent the afternoon tidying our bedrooms so we'd be allowed to watch the fireworks."

"You haven't been kayaking since?"

"The next time Trent went to the boat shed, the hole had

been repaired and there was a padlock on the door." And while Trent had been angry, she and Tiffy had been relieved.

"Yet you work at a rowing club, renting kayaks and canoes and sailing dinghies to anyone who comes in." There was a definite smile in Logan's tone.

"I fit them each with an appropriate high-spec life jacket and give them all a detailed safety briefing. And I keep watch." She crossed her arms over her chest.

"And does Hannah do that as well? And whoever manages the club on your days off?"

"Of course." She wouldn't work at the rowing club if they didn't keep the highest safety standards. That was one reason she'd accepted the role when Hannah offered it—to make sure no one had a repeat of her experience. And no one had.

"So let's go kayaking. You're older and stronger, and you're aware of the risks."

"Are you saying nothing will go wrong?" Because no one could make that kind of guarantee.

"I'm saying it's less likely. I've checked the forecast. Tomorrow looks good. Why not?"

Why not indeed.

She'd do it.

She inhaled a deep breath of determination. "Okay. I'll come kayaking with you."

His answering smile was brighter than the fireworks.

CHAPTER THIRTEEN

Logan and Tabitha had the kitchen and guest rooms shipshape and Bristol fashion before eleven on Saturday morning . . . right on schedule. Logan's schedule. Now he just had to persuade Tabitha. She'd said yes to the kayak trip when they talked about the boat shed, but that didn't mean she was going to say yes now. That would be too easy. And nothing about his pursuit of Tabitha Thomas had been easy.

Where was she?

In the kitchen, as usual. Today she was standing in front of the open pantry doors as if meditating on the contents. Better get in quick, before she started cooking or baking.

"Hey, Tabitha." He came up behind her and hugged her around the waist. "It's a perfect day for kayaking. How about it?"

She turned in his arms to face him, and he gave her a quick kiss.

"I would like to, but . . ."

He'd known there'd be a "but."

"Rhonda Ingalls asked if I'd mind whipping up a pan of lasagna for—"

Logan silenced her with another kiss, a little longer this

time. "Stop. I don't need to know. How about we kayak this afternoon and I help you bake lasagna this evening. Would that work?"

"I was going to make a double batch, so we could have some for dinner as well." She didn't come out and ask if he knew how to make lasagna, but something inside told him she was thinking it.

"Even better. I love lasagna, and I make a mean Bolognese sauce. Do you have mince in that giant freezer of yours?" She had that blank look again, the look that said they were divided by a common language. "Ground beef. Do you have any ground beef in your giant freezer?"

"Of course."

"Then we can go kayaking while it defrosts. I swear the sauce tastes better if the meat has defrosted naturally, not been blasted in the microwave."

"Leah says the same thing." Her cute half-smile said she was coming around to his suggestion.

"Then we're sorted. You come kayaking with me now. I'll organize a picnic lunch, and I'll help you make lasagna for dinner." He released her, stepped back, and held out a hand.

"Deal." She shook his hand and gave him a real smile, one that stretched all the way from her luscious lips to her sparkling eyes.

Whew. Operation First Date was a go. Not that he was calling it a date, because that might scare her off. He still had no idea why she'd gone from frozen to flirty in only a few days, but he wasn't going to ask awkward questions which might have awkward answers.

Half an hour later, they were pushing off from the rowing club jetty in a smart double kayak, both wearing top-of-the-line hi-vis life jackets and transporting a sturdy picnic basket full of deli delights, courtesy of Leah and her organics store. He'd been worried that Tabitha might be afraid of the water to the point she didn't want to get in the kayak, but she'd managed to clamber in and keep her balance with no sign of fear. There was a touch of tension in her shoulders, but that could be the water, the kayak, or him. Hopefully not him.

"Let's head toward that bay for lunch." Logan pointed his paddle to a sandy stretch over to their left. It had taken him around an hour to get there on his own, so should only take forty minutes or so with two of them paddling. Not too far, but still time for Tabitha to acclimatize. Time to talk.

"Okay."

"I love getting out in nature like this. I'm not a fan of living in cities where nature is confined to parks." As it had been in most of the places he'd lived as a child.

"I don't think I could live in a city like that."

"Even though you've lived on the lakefront your entire life and haven't explored the lake for the last fifteen years?"

"I've never needed to get out on the water to feel close to nature. I can see across the lake, to where the mountains reach the sky. There's something special about that." Tabitha stopped paddling and allowed her paddle to trail in the lake as she leaned back and admired the sky.

"Agreed." Logan could already see her shoulders softening as her tension trickled away. She didn't appear to have any residual fear of water.

"How can you afford to travel so much when you don't have a regular job?" Tabitha asked.

"I have four regular jobs—seasonal jobs. Besides, I don't need a lot. I don't have any debt, I don't have anyone to support except myself, and I don't need a heap of stuff. Stuff just ties people down." Like the inn tied Tabitha to Trinity Lakes. If only she could see it.

"No debt?" she asked. "No student loans?"

"Football scholarships." And a generous allowance from his parents.

"It must have been a good scholarship."

"Better than most." Because he was a better kicker than most. Some American college football players couldn't kick a ball over the posts from straight in front. Even in high school, he could get the ball over the posts from pretty much anywhere in his half.

"Didn't you get drafted into the NFL? What happened?"

"I was a fifth-round draft pick but blew out my ankle early in my first season." At least they'd covered his medical bills and rehab.

"Were you disappointed?" Tabby sounded concerned.

"Not as much as I should have been. I think that's when I realized football was a means to an end. It wasn't where I was meant to be." It wasn't where God wanted him, but he and Tabby had never talked about their faith. Maybe now was the time to start.

"And traveling the globe, working seasonal jobs is?" Her curious tone told him this was an honest question, not an accusation.

"For today, yes. That might change. I have to trust God will make that clear to me when the time comes." And that he wouldn't be so attached to a position or place or person that he'd be reluctant to move on when the call came.

Tabby sat back in the kayak, as if contemplating what he'd said.

They drifted into the sandy bay Logan had pointed out, climbed out of the kayak, and pulled it up on the shore. It might have been fifteen years since Tabby had paddled a kayak, but she had the technique and confidence of someone born to water.

Logan grabbed the picnic basket and blanket, which he unfurled with a flourish and laid on the sand, then unpacked a combination of cheese, crackers, cold meats, chopped vegetables, fresh bread, and dips. Leah had outdone herself—no doubt because he'd told her it was all for Tabitha.

"Bon appétit," he said.

"Will you say the blessing?" Tabitha asked, as though it was some kind of test.

"Of course." Logan bowed his head and closed his eyes. "Lord, we thank You for bringing us here together safely, and we thank You for the food we have before us. May You bless it to our bodies and keep us safe as we serve You. Amen."

"Amen."

Logan opened his eyes to find Tabitha giving him an assessing look.

"Is this a date?" she asked.

"If you'd like it to be a date, then yes. It's a date. But if you just want to have a picnic as friends . . . well, it could be that as well." He was an adult. He'd faced rejection before, and he'd face it again. He'd cope.

"Did you date during high school?"

"Hardly." He choked back a laugh. "I went to a boys-only Anglican high school in New Zealand."

"Anglican?" Her nose wrinkled in an adorable look of confusion.

"Anglican is Church of England. Americans call it Episcopalian. A lot of the boarding schools in New Zealand were set up by the Anglican church back in the day to provide kids who lived in remote areas with a secondary education."

"And they were all single-sex schools?"

"Yes, although a lot of the boys' schools accept girls in the higher years."

"So no girls in school." Tabitha selected a cracker from the basket and added a wedge of cheese. "What about college? You dated Tiffany."

"Your sister? We never dated." Trent had never given him grief about dating Tiffany. Tabitha was another story—he couldn't forget Trent's "do not date my sister" lecture in relation to Tabitha.

"She said you did." Her words were flat, perhaps deliberately flat, as if she was trying not to sound as though she was accusing him of something.

"We went out once. That's a date. Not dating. Not a relationship." Semantics, maybe. But Logan did not want Tabitha thinking she was second-best to her sister.

"So is this our first date?"

"This is our second date, if you count you inviting me to explore the boat shed with you." He winked, and she gave an exaggerated eye roll. "Now, let's enjoy the picnic Leah put together for us."

"This is delicious." Tabby selected a stick of celery and took a scoop of the smoked salmon dip. "I'd love to make food like this, but it's not exactly breakfast food."

"What would you like to make?" She was a great cook—he'd never had a bad or even a so-so meal at the inn.

Logan leaned back against the side of the kayak as she described a range of recipes, all of which would make fabulous finger food.

If it wasn't for the fact he'd just stuffed himself on Trinity Organics' finest, he'd want to sample all the delicacies Tabitha described.

She might not have admitted it to herself, but she was sold on turning the boat shed into a café or restaurant or event venue. Was that her secret dream?

Lord, please help Tabby to hear You. Please help her discover Your will for her life. Please help her move on from Trinity Lakes if that's what You have for her. And if moving on from her means moving on from me, please give me the strength to let her go.

CHAPTER FOURTEEN

Turn, fold, punch. Tabby always found kneading bread therapeutic. Turn, fold, punch. Turn, fold, punch. She looked up as Dad walked into the kitchen, holding a large envelope.

"Here's the report from the engineers."

"An actual paper report? Not an email?" Logan looked up from his position on the barstool, e-reader in his hand.

"A physical report. With original signatures, pen on paper. The kind the council can't possibly find fault with." Dad placed the envelope on the kitchen counter with a grim smile. "Because they're not going to like this, and I don't want to give them any reason to discount or ignore the findings."

"What does it say? Is the boat shed built on a floodplain?" Logan placed his e-reader on the counter.

"Short answer, no. The engineers found no evidence to suggest that any part of the Lake Wainscott foreshore is part of a floodplain." Dad took a seat at the kitchen counter and folded his arms.

"Then why was the land zoned as a floodplain in the first

place?" Tabby continued kneading, not wanting to let the dough rest too long. Turn, fold, punch. "There must be something."

Logan flipped through the report. "This is weird. It looks as though whoever made the original decision based it entirely on the fact that the town is built on a river." He flicked through a few more pages. "The original papers don't include any of the usual tests for a floodplain. The engineers have now run those tests—you can read the details yourself, later—and Trinity Lakes has come up clean."

"That doesn't tell us why it was zoned as a floodplain."

"I think Logan's earlier theory must have been right." Dad closed the report and rested his hand on top. "I think it had something do to with the property developer."

"Property developer? Why? Gran didn't need money."

"No . . ." Something in Dad's tone told Tabby he was holding back information.

"Then why did she consider selling?" Surely she had a reason.

"We had you three." Dad let out a long breath. "You were two months premature—not uncommon for multiple births—and that meant a long stay in the neonatal unit."

"That can't have been cheap," Logan said. "I remember my mother talking about her sticker shock when I was born in Florida. The hospital bill was thousands, and that was for a single healthy baby and only one night in hospital."

"Didn't you and Mom have insurance?" Tabby asked. Turn, fold, punch. The surface of the dough was turning shiny.

"Not enough," Dad said. "It covered your birth and hospital costs, but that's all."

"So your grandmother put the land on the market to cover the difference." Logan reached for the report and flicked through it.

"A property developer offered your grandmother a lot of

money." Dad's tone was grim. "They wanted to build lakefront high-rise apartments and a shopping mall."

"Gran would have hated that." Tabby shaped the dough into a ball. It held its shape. Good. "Is that why she didn't sell?"

"Your grandmother was determined to protect her view of the lake and the feel of the town."

"And keep the boat shed?" Tabby tipped the dough into a bowl and covered it with a clean tea towel.

"Maybe. Anyway, the decision was taken out of her hands. The buyer withdrew their offer."

"Did they say why?" Tabby positioned the bowl in a patch of sunshine streaming across the counter.

"I don't remember. I was in NICU with you three."

Oh. Yeah. That minor detail.

"Then Martha called to say she'd had another offer."

"Wayne Gilbertson?" Hannah's father would have been the only person in town with enough money to outbid a property developer.

"He didn't offer nearly as much, but it was enough to cover the medical bills with a little left over, and it meant the inn would still have lake views."

"So Martha made the decision on her own?" Logan asked.

"It was her property and her decision. I offered advice when asked, but I was barely surviving myself." Dad sounded tired, as though even remembering took him back to those difficult days.

So Gran was able to keep the Lakeview Inn, Dad had somewhere to live and someone to help him raise Tabby and her siblings, and Trinity Lakes hadn't been transformed from a sleepy small town into a tacky tourist destination.

All because the land was zoned as a floodplain.

———

LOGAN BROUGHT the last load of dirty sheets downstairs and piled them into the laundry basket, then loaded and set the machine. "Tabby, what time are tonight's guests checking in?"

"Around four." She rolled the last of the dry towels and stacked them on the cleaning trolley.

"Now we've got the engineer's report, how about we go for a walk along the lakefront? I'd like to see what the boat shed looks like from further around." Although he'd take any excuse for a romantic lakefront walk with Tabitha.

"So we can think about what we might want to add or change? I like that idea."

Fifteen minutes later, they'd loaded and set the washer and dryer, cleaned the kitchen, and turned the dishwasher on.

Logan took Tabitha's hand as they walked down the front path to the lakefront boardwalk.

"Logan, do you ever plan to settle down?" Tabitha asked.

He was tempted to say "one day," his usual pat answer, but something in Tabitha's expression told him that would be the wrong response. No surprise there. Tabitha was reliable. Trustworthy. Responsible. She'd lived in the same small town her entire life.

"I'm not used to staying in one place. Never have been. I guess I take after my parents, the way you take after your dad." Logan hadn't thought about it before now, but Tabby had a lot in common with her father. Both were faithful Christians who worked hard and used their talents to serve their community. His parents worked hard. There the similarity ended.

"Your parents . . ." Tabitha gestured for him to say more.

"My parents met while they were at university and married soon after they graduated. They worked in New Zealand for a couple of years, then went to London to do the big OE."

"OE? What's that?"

"Overseas experience. Young people go to London for a couple of years to travel and see the world." He paused. How would his life have been different if Mum and Dad had done the traditional Kiwi thing—lived in a cramped flat in Shepherd's Bush and worked shifts in some minimum-wage service job? He'd never know.

"Sounds like fun."

"Dad got an architecture job with a big construction firm. He worked in London for a couple of years, then they sent him to Aussie because they needed someone on-site quickly and didn't have time to figure out work visas ."

That had been the start. Dad had quickly established himself as someone who could take charge of the difficult projects, and who was prepared to move city or country with little or no notice.

"He got offered a role in Florida—where I was born—then Singapore. The jobs never lasted long—maybe six months, maybe a year." It was all second nature to him, but Tabby had the wide-eyed look of someone who couldn't imagine living and working in multiple countries.

"How many places have you lived?"

"Eight? Ten? We went back to Singapore when I was about ten, but I'd lived in London, Christchurch, and a couple of cities in China before then." Now he thought about it, living in so many countries seemed unbelievable.

"What did you do for school?"

"A combination of regular school and international schools, depending on where we were living. Then boarding school." Five years at boarding school in Auckland had been the longest he'd lived anywhere.

Tabby was silent, and the look on her face said she was processing.

"So where's your hometown?"

Logan had to laugh. "Hometown" was such an American concept. "Auckland, I guess. That's where I went to high school, and that's where my mother's family lives, so I've spent more time there than anywhere except Washington."

"Didn't that bother you?" Tabby asked.

"As a child, I thought moving all the time was normal. I was probably six or seven before I noticed other families didn't move once or twice a year." The realization that other people lived in one house and went to one school and saw their grandparents and cousins more often than every other Christmas hit hard.

"So how many states have you visited?"

"I lost count. Please don't make me list them." He wasn't trying to boast.

"I've barely left Washington. Humor me."

"Okay. Disneyland in California and Florida. New York, and Washington, DC, on obligatory tourist visits. You know the kind. White House, Times Square—"

"Where else?"

"I have photographs of myself at Mt. Rushmore, Devil's Tower, the Grand Canyon, Delicate Arch, and Four Corners. So that's South Dakota, Wyoming, Utah, Arizona, New Mexico, and . . . I can't remember."

"Colorado."

"If you say so."

"If you could live anywhere you've visited, where would you choose?"

She probably expected him to say something exotic or foreign or fun, but that wouldn't be the truth.

"I'd choose right here. Trinity Lakes, Washington." Logan stopped walking and pulled Tabitha into a loose hug.

"Here?" Her tone told him she didn't believe him. "Why here, of all places?"

Because she was here. Because this was the first place he'd felt at home since . . . since he couldn't remember. The only place he felt at home. She met his gaze, and he couldn't stop himself from dropping a quick kiss on her inviting lips.

"Because Washington's trees and lakes and mountains remind me of New Zealand, and the weather is good. Not too hot, not too cold." That was close enough to the truth to be honest, yet not so honest that he'd scare her away. "What about you? If you could travel anywhere in the world, where would you go?"

She didn't hesitate.

"Paris." The city of love. She didn't say it, but she didn't have to. He could see it in her far-off gaze, hear it in the yearning in her voice. "And Rome. I've heard the food in Italy is amazing."

She wasn't wrong.

"And if I'm thinking about food, Greece and Japan and Thailand and . . . oh, all the places." Her voice trailed off as if she was losing herself in dreams of foreign food.

So Tabitha Thomas was a foodie with dreams of travel. Who knew.

———

TABBY ARRIVED at the rowing club on Monday afternoon to find Hannah pacing like a prowling panther.

"Becky tells me she saw you and Logan walking along the lakefront together." Hannah gave Tabby a look that could have frozen Lake Gilbertson on the Fourth of July. "She said you were holding hands and looking all cozy together and she swears he kissed you." Hannah's tone was indignant, but Tabby couldn't tell if her indignation was because Tabby hadn't told Hannah . . . or because Becky had.

And they weren't dating.

Not really. Not properly. Not officially.

"Yes, but—"

"You told Becky you're dating your hot houseguest, but you didn't tell me?"

"I didn't tell Becky. And I haven't seen you for over a week, so when was I supposed to tell you?" Typical small-town gossip.

"There's this little invention called the telephone." Hannah mimicked making a phone call. "You could have called."

"This shouldn't be a surprise." Tabby bent down to stow her purse behind the reception desk. "You're the one who's been teasing me since he arrived in town. And you're the one who hired us the kayaks for our first date."

"You didn't tell me that was a date!" Hannah raised her hands and looked heavenward as though pleading for divine assistance. "I know you've been spending all your spare time with him, but you'd told me you weren't dating because he's not a Christian."

"Turns out he is a Christian." Tabby rearranged the pens on the desk, pens that didn't need rearranging.

"So I figured. I'll forgive you for not telling me. As long as you tell me everything that happened, starting with the kayaking date."

Tabby shared the basics of their boat shed and kayaking dates—assuming the boat shed was a date, given she'd asked Logan. But she wasn't going to tell Hannah everything. Especially not the kissing. The very nice kissing.

"You're blushing. Becky was right. He kissed you. When? Where? Why didn't you tell me?"

They were not questions Tabby was willing to answer. Not that she needed to. Hannah would see the answer in her heated checks. "I guess the reason I didn't tell you is because I don't want the gossips getting hold of it."

"I don't gossip. And if you wanted to keep it a secret, you shouldn't have taken a romantic lakeside walk where the Rhondas could see you, so what's your problem?"

"I don't know if it's going to last. Long-distance relationships and all that. And I don't want everyone feeling sorry for me when he leaves."

Because everyone left. Growing up, it had been Tabby and Tiffy and Trent . . . then Tiffy and Trent left, while Tabby stayed in Trinity Lakes. Her high school boyfriend left for college then infamously dumped her by text message. The other teens she'd been friendly with in high school had all left. Gran died. The fact that Tabby had any friends now was mostly due to Hannah befriending her, employing her, and dragging her to book club and church and every possible community event.

"Logan might not leave."

"Of course he'll leave. He's leaving for summer camp in about three weeks."

"What are his plans after camp?"

"I guess he'll be heading off who knows where for his next job." They hadn't discussed where he was going after his time at Camp Trinity. There was no reason to ask before they had started dating—if that was what they were doing—and now they were? She didn't want to think about Logan leaving. She'd rather pretend he would stay here forever.

"Do you think he might stay?"

"Why would he? Most people want more out of life than a low-wage job in a tiny tourist town in the back end of Washington."

"Thanks, Tabby. Nice to know what you really think of me and the rowing club." Hannah's wink and wry smile said she knew Tabby's comment wasn't personal.

"Sorry. I'm venting."

"Forgiven. I know you didn't mean it how it sounded." Hannah paused and looked down at her hands, flexing her fingers as if she was admiring a nonexistent manicure. "Have you thought of leaving?"

"With Logan? Of course not. That would be—"

"Not with Logan. Just you. You've never left Trinity Lakes, never been to college, never been anywhere."

Thanks, Hannah. Rub it in.

"Speaking of leaving, I have to fly. Granny Gracie said she'd drop in with a batch of brownies for the young mother's group meeting here tomorrow. Can you hide them, please? I don't want the teens devouring them."

"I'll lock them in my drawer." Tabby straightened the pile of invoices she needed to key into the system this afternoon.

"Thank you. Bye!" Hannah almost skipped out of the club. She must be meeting Joel.

Tabby considered Hannah's words as she coded invoices. She'd love to leave, to travel, but how? She had so many responsibilities. Running the inn. Working for Hannah. Renovating Gran's rooms. Planning the renovations on the boat shed. She couldn't leave.

"Penny for them."

Tabby looked up to find Grannie Gracie standing at the reception desk, holding a large cake tin. Tabby hadn't even heard the door open.

"Are those the brownies I'm supposed to hide?"

"They are." Grannie Gracie passed the container to Tabby. "You can have one if you tell me what you were concentrating on so hard that you didn't hear me come in. I'm sure it wasn't that paperwork."

"Nothing in particular." Tabby hid the brownies at the bottom of the stationery drawer, where no one would look for them.

"Don't prevaricate with me, young lady. I promised your dear grandmother I'd look out for you, so you can't say 'nothing' and expect me to believe you." Grannie Gracie might sound sweet, but she and Gran shared the same steel backbone.

Which meant Tabby could share her burdens now or share them later, but she would have to share. "Something Hannah said about leaving Trinity Lakes got me thinking about all my responsibilities, the reasons I can't leave—the inn, my job here, baking for church."

"None of those are reasons to stay if you want to go to college or something." Grannie Gracie softened her tone. "Hannah could hire someone else. So could your father."

"What about the cooking and baking for church? Someone has to do it. You can't do it all."

"And neither can you, my dear."

"Gran always did it. I want to carry on, in her memory." And if Tabby didn't run the inn, who would?

"Your grandmother is with Jesus now. It might be time for someone else to take over some of her roles."

"Who? No one else has volunteered to help."

"Rhonda Ingalls says you say yes to anything as soon as she asks. I'm sure Pastor Ladan would say the same. You're not giving anyone else the chance."

"They could offer." She knew she sounded defensive, but really. If anyone wanted to help, all they had to do was tell her. Or Rhonda. Or Pastor Ladan. Or Mrs. Ladan.

"Did it ever occur to you that doing something that isn't your calling might be preventing someone else from stepping up to their own calling?"

Honestly, that hadn't occurred to her. Surely if someone had a calling, they'd say something. Surely. "Has someone said something to you?"

"No, but your grandmother would be worried about you. I'm worried about you."

"Why would you be worried?"

"It sounds like you're doing too much. Always putting everyone else first. Not taking care of yourself."

"It's what Gran would have done. What Gran did."

"Yes, but that was her calling. She lived to cook, to feed others. Her love language was acts of service. You . . . I've been wondering for a while if you're taking over her volunteer roles for the wrong reasons."

"Surely what matters is that we feed the hungry, like Jesus said."

"We should serve out of love, not obligation."

"You're saying I serve out of obligation?"

"Only you can answer that. Is spending all your spare time cooking for other people your God-given calling? If it is, then I withdraw my comments. But if it isn't, then you're denying someone the opportunity to practice obedience. Worse, you're being disobedient yourself."

"I work for Hannah. I manage the inn. I don't feel any 'calling' to do anything else."

Grannie Gracie snorted. Not a polite huff, but an actual snort, like a pig. "Of course you don't. You barely give yourself time to breathe, let alone time to be still and listen to God."

You're always working. You need to give yourself time to relax, to rest, to think. Logan's words echoed through her mind.

Yes, she was always busy. There was always so much to get done. The inn, work, church. Baking cookies for children's church. Delivering casseroles to shut-ins and new parents and bereaved widows and widowers. Gran always said it was a privilege to serve, and it was even more of a privilege to take over Gran's acts of service.

"You need to learn to say no. Give yourself some space in your life so you have space to say yes when the right opportunity presents itself. As I'm sure it will."

The door opened behind Grannie Gracie. Several teens tumbled in and headed for the locker rooms.

"And that's my cue to leave. I'll leave you to think on what I've said." Gracie gave a ladylike wave and swanned out of the door.

So Gran had tasked Gracie with looking out for Tabby? That wasn't a surprise—they'd been friends for as long as Tabby could remember. Gran had even named her daughter—Tabby's mother—after her best friend.

What was a surprise was that Grannie Gracie was questioning Tabby's work and even her motives. Was she serving for the right reasons? She'd never stopped to think. She'd just continued to serve the way Gran always had.

Maybe Gracie was right. Maybe it was time to consider her own calling.

CHAPTER FIFTEEN

Another day, another morning, another breakfast for the guests. Another day of tasks and to-dos and putting others first, another day of not considering her calling. Tabby stood at the kitchen island, slicing cold potatoes for today's breakfast of Spanish frittata with homemade salsa. Guests raved about her frittata, prepared according to Gran's age-old recipe, and which she could probably prepare with her eyes closed after making it once a week for the last four years.

Yes, she was grateful she had a job. Two jobs, in fact. But there were days when it was easy to feel grateful and days when it wasn't so easy. Days when she'd rather be doing something else. Following Gran's dream. Following her own dreams. Following Logan.

Logan, who was going to leave. She'd resented him coming to stay, and now she was going to resent him leaving for summer camp. Goodness. His time here was already more than half over.

"Morning, honey." Dad entered the kitchen and poured himself a cup of coffee from the carafe in the coffee machine.

"Morning. Any plans for today?" Enough of the maudlin self-reflection. Time to turn on contented Tabby.

"Taxes are done, so I was thinking we could go over to the boat shed and see what it looks like. Now we know the land is ours, we should find out if the building is salvageable and saleable." He poured himself a coffee and leaned against the counter.

Tabby stopped slicing and turned to face her father. "Sell the boat shed?"

"Like I said, it's your decision. Yours and Tiffy's and Trent's." Dad waved his hand, as though brushing her words away. "But you need to know what state the building is in first. What needs doing."

"A lot." Logan joined Dad on a stool at the kitchen counter. "Tabby and I had a look inside a few days ago, before the report arrived. It needs a new interior floor—there's a lot of damp, which suggests rotten floorboards. A full fit-out, new plumbing, new wiring to bring it up to code . . ." Logan recited the list as he grabbed granola from the pantry and milk from the fridge.

"All that will depend on what the boat shed is going to be used for, which would be up to the buyer." Dad took a long draw of his coffee.

"I don't want to sell." Tabby's words were louder, sharper, more forceful than she'd intended. She softened her tone. "I want to keep it."

"Why?" Dad helped himself to a bowl of granola.

"I've always loved the boat shed." It had fascinated her—partly because of the location, and partly because it was off-limits. That had appealed to her adventurous side, the side she rarely let loose. Being adventurous was dangerous, reckless, risky. Not safe. Not sensible. Not responsible.

"You can love it without wanting to keep it." Dad took a seat at the kitchen counter with his coffee and granola.

"Remember how Gran used to talk about having a catering

business?" Tabby scraped the potatoes into a large pan and switched to dicing an onion. "The boat shed would be the perfect location."

"I remember your grandmother discussing that with me. At the time, I didn't realize she owned the land and building." He took a mouthful of granola.

"I found her scrapbook. It's full of decorating ideas for a café or something similar—table settings, crockery, cutlery, chairs." She mixed most of the onion with the potatoes, added a dash of freshly ground black pepper, added the egg, covered the pan, and set it on a low heat.

"A lot of the decorating ideas are straight out of the eighties—dark wood paneling and fluoro Formica." Logan sounded slightly disgusted, as though he'd be happy for those decorating ideas to stay in the 1980s. He wasn't wrong.

"Logan found boxes and boxes of fancy china, the kind people use for a fancy afternoon tea." Tabby dug in the fridge and located the fresh tomatoes she'd bought from Leah on her way home from work yesterday. "I think something rustic could work well."

"Something that takes advantage of the character of the building?" Dad asked between mouthfuls.

"Yes, but with modern appliances and plumbing and electricity. All of which is going to add up to more money than we have." The trust owned the inn and boat shed outright, and the inn covered costs and provided enough profit to cover Tiffy and Trent's dorm fees through college, but there wasn't money to spare for taking on a new project.

"You could use your college fund." Dad rested his spoon in the now-empty bowl.

"College fund?" Tabby stopped chopping the tomatoes and turned to face her father. "What college fund?"

"Your grandmother set up college funds for each of you

when you were born. She gave Trent and Tiffany theirs when they passed their freshman year."

"Only when they passed?" Logan asked, his tone hiding a hint of humor Tabby hoped Dad didn't hear.

"Let's say she wasn't sure Trent was going to college for the right reasons."

"Wise woman." Logan took a mouthful of his cereal.

"Anyway, all those checks your grandmother sent Tiffy and Trent during college? She always put the same amount into your account. She didn't want to treat you differently."

"Why didn't she tell me?" Tabby had thought she and Gran had shared everything, yet now Tabby was finding yet one more thing Gran hadn't shared. "And why didn't you tell me?"

"She didn't want you going to college just for the money. If you didn't go to college, then she wanted you to use the money to invest in something for your future. Something like college or buying a house or going on the mission field. Or investing in a business."

"A business like the boat shed?" Tabby scraped the diced onion and chopped tomatoes into a bowl, added a dash of black pepper and a splash of hot sauce, then stirred.

"As long as you can show that renovating the boat shed is an investment with a reasonable chance of providing a financial return." He took a long sip of coffee and looked over the cup at her. "It's simply good stewardship. Making good use of our time, talents, and resources."

"I can make it work." She was sure she could. Her deepest dream—travel—would remain a dream. She couldn't leave. She was needed here, in Trinity.

"From what Logan's discovered, you'll need to sort out the zoning first."

"That means putting in an application for a zoning change with the city," Logan said. "I looked online. I found the process for getting land designated as a floodplain, but nothing to get it undesignated—if that's even the word. It could take a while."

"The gears of city hall grind exceedingly slowly, as several of my clients have unhappily informed me." Dad stretched his arms behind his head.

"What about permits?" Logan asked.

"There's not much point in applying for permits until you know the outcome of the rezoning application."

"This could take forever." So much for the boat shed opening by summer. She gave the salsa a final stir and checked on the frittata. Almost done.

"Months, at least. Start with applying for the zoning change." Dad folded his hands on the counter.

"In the meantime, we can renovate your grandmother's bedroom and bathroom," Logan said.

We. Did that mean Logan was planning on staying in the USA? In Trinity Lakes?

"You can work up your plans. Figure out what you want to do, how much it's going to cost, and what permits you're going to need. A business plan."

"Why do I need a business plan? You said I could use the college fund." How much was in this mysterious college fund? She didn't want to ask in front of Logan in case the figure was embarrassingly large . . . or embarrassingly small. "Will I need a loan from the bank on top of my college fund?"

"Maybe. Maybe not." Dad leaned back. "We won't know until you've worked up the plan and costed the project. Then you'll have to get your siblings onboard with the project, given you're each equal owners in the boat shed."

"Even if I'm paying for all the renovations?"

"There's little point renovating the building if Tiffy and Trent want to sell," Dad said.

"Neither of them will want the responsibility," Logan said. "They might think it's easier to sell."

"But you wouldn't mind if I turned the boat shed into a business?" Tabby asked her father.

"Honey, your grandmother and I always knew it was never your calling to run the B&B."

"Someone has to do it." Tabby washed her hands and wiped down the kitchen counters so everything would look perfect when the guests came in.

"That someone doesn't have to be you."

"Are you saying I haven't done a good job?" A shot of pain ran through her at the thought.

"You do a great job, but I'm not convinced the inn is where you're meant to be. This was Martha's calling. She lived to cook, to feed others. Her love language was acts of service. You . . . I worry that you're doing this out of obligation and love for your grandmother, not out of a God-given sense of purpose and love for the people you're serving."

"I enjoy cooking breakfasts and running the inn."

Logan looked at her with raised eyebrows. Yes, she enjoyed cooking breakfasts, but she wanted to do more. And he knew it.

"You do great breakfasts," Dad said. "But you also do great hors d'oeuvres and finger food, casseroles and cakes. And I would never have risked my life by saying this when your grandmother was still alive, but your Thanksgiving turkey ran circles around hers." He looked at Logan as if seeking confirmation.

"He's right. Your turkey and stuffing are amazing."

"If you want to live here and manage the B&B, it's yours . . . well, yours and Trent's and Tiffy's. But you do too much already. You can't do everything. If you decide to turn the boat shed into a business, you might need to give up something else."

Give something up? But what?

CHAPTER SIXTEEN

Over the next two weeks, Logan spent his spare time researching and preparing a rezoning request for the city council. The process resulted in more crossed eyes and screwed-up paper than boarding school at exam time, but he eventually got the paperwork completed and filed with a little help from Mr. Thomas, a little less from Tabitha, and none at all from Tiffy or Trent.

Once he'd hand-delivered the application, it was a case of sitting back and waiting, because he'd gotten the impression that the city council's response would be somewhat slower than sloth-like.

Now he could focus on spending enough time at the gym to rebuild the strength in his ankle—but not so much that he over-stressed it and put a damper on the healing process—and working with Tabby to empty and renovate her grandmother's bedroom, so that could be made available to summer guests.

But today was Saturday, and the inn's Australian guests were staying for a full week, which meant no one needed to be around to check in new guests.

Saturday morning dawned bright and clear, which was an

answer to prayer because he and Tabby were headed to a local football game this afternoon. But not a regular football game.

"So what's the big deal about this game?" Logan asked as Tabitha parked her jeep in the high school car park.

"It's the annual Anzac game—Anzacs vs. Americans." Anzac Day was the Australian and New Zealand equivalent of Memorial Day.

"Why Anzacs?" Logan caught Tabitha's hand as she led them toward the football field.

"Mr. Kennedy—he's the high school principal—he and Mrs. Kennedy taught in Australia for a few years and brought back some of the culture and history. But it's not a holiday here, so we have the game the first Saturday after actual Anzac Day."

He'd spent several holidays and vacations in Trinity over the years, but he'd never visited in late April and never stopped to consider why this small town in Washington had so many Australian residents and visitors.

"Why Aussie rules? Australian Rules football. I would've thought rugby would have been more of an Anzac game." Or cricket.

"I think that's the Kennedy influence again. Do you play this kind of football, or just American football?"

"I've never played Aussie rules. I grew up playing rugby, then switched to American football in college. That didn't stop Caleb trying to sign me up to play in today's game."

"With your ankle?" Tabby laughed.

"I guess he heard my accent and assumed I could play. Didn't see I've still got strapping on my ankle and didn't ask if I played the game."

"How is your ankle? You haven't worn that boot thing in ages, and you're not limping or anything."

"It's a lot better—not good enough to risk playing football or walk a few hundred miles, but good enough for everyday activities."

"Good enough for camp?" There was a shade of hopefulness in her words. Was she hoping he'd be fit enough to head off to summer camp . . . or that he wouldn't be?

"Adam has cleared me for camp as long as I don't play football or do anything else that could potentially jar my ankle." And he'd been strangely disappointed by Adam's appraisal.

They found seats on the top row of the bleachers behind one set of goalposts just as the teams marched onto the field—the Anzacs in an Australian kit of green and gold, and the Americans in red, white, and blue.

The high school band marched out onto the field, and the crowd hushed. A single trumpet player stepped forward and raised his instrument to his lips.

The poignant notes of the "Last Post" rang through the bleachers, followed by the traditional minute of silence, and "Reveille." Logan recognized both from the Anzac Day services he'd attended as a teenager at boarding school.

Then the crowd sang as the band played the national anthems. The band marched off the field, and everyone sat down as the captains of each team approached the referee for the coin toss. The players dispersed, and it looked as though the Anzacs were playing toward them in the first half.

"Do you have any idea of the rules?" Logan asked.

"All I know is each team has to get the ball to their goal line —like in American football—but the same team plays the whole game. There's no offense or defense or special teams."

"That's pretty much all I know as well."

The whistle blew, and a dozen men scrambled for the ball.

"Tabitha Thomas, is that you?"

Tabby turned in the direction of the call.

A tall, skinny woman with dark hair swanned up the stairs, all slim-fitting designer jeans and picture-perfect makeup, her hair in an immaculate ponytail. She might have been pretty if she'd smiled.

"How are you, Kyla?" Tabby's tone turned icy polite.

"Outstanding." Kyla pivoted toward Logan and turned on a megawatt smile. "We haven't met. I'm Kyla Ferguson."

"Oh, sorry," Tabitha said. "This is Logan. He's staying at the inn. Logan, meet Kyla."

"Nice to meet you." He offered Kyla his hand to shake.

Kyla turned toward the field and let out an eardrum-shattering whistle. "Go Anzacs!"

"Aren't you supposed to cheer for the local team?" Logan asked.

Kyla gave him a saccharine smile. "Not anymore. I am Team Caleb till death us do part." She flashed her ring finger in front of Logan's face, and he caught a glimpse of something gold and gaudy. Beside him, Tabby stiffened.

"You and Caleb are engaged? Congratulations."

"Yes, Caleb proposed. He finally got the hint." Kyla waved her ring in front of Tabitha so she could supply the requisite oohs and aahs.

"When's the big day?" Not that Logan was interested, but it was polite to ask. The engagement must be recent, because Logan had seen Caleb in the gym on Wednesday, and he hadn't said anything.

"I'm planning a November wedding. I'm sure Caleb will agree." Kyla waved her hand as if to imply that of course Caleb would agree with her. "Which is why I wanted to talk to you. I heard you were considering converting the old boat shed into an event venue."

"We're looking into it." Tabby's tone was somewhat distant.

"The boat shed would make an excellent wedding venue, with the sun over the water at sunset."

Tabitha didn't respond, even though that was exactly what they'd both thought.

"I'd like to get married there. You can book me in as your first client."

"We don't know if we can get the boat shed up and running by November," Tabby said. "We need to get the land rezoned, and to get permits approved."

"I'm sure God will make sure everything falls into place so I can have a waterfront wedding."

This Kyla had quite the ego.

Tabby let loose a cheer for the home team, who were all jumping around and hugging each other. They must have scored.

"It's such a shame you have to run the inn and work for Hannah." Kyla's words dripped with fake sympathy. "Between that and church, you can't have any spare time for a social life."

"I'm sure you have the same challenge, given the amount of time you put into organizing the youth group." Tabitha's tone matched Kyla's in sincerity. "And did I hear you'll be volunteering at Camp Trinity over the summer?"

"Of course. I adore working with our youth."

"Logan has signed up to be a camp counselor as well."

"I'll look forward to working with you." In the same way as he'd look forward to a dental appointment.

"I'll miss him when he leaves." Tabitha took his hand and leaned against his shoulder.

Logan gave Tabitha's hand a squeeze. She squeezed back, and held their joined hands up to Kyla.

"You're dating?" Kyla's tone held such obvious disbelief that Logan was insulted on Tabitha's behalf. Sure, they'd only been on one official date—two, if you counted today's game—but that was still dating.

"For a little while." She stretched "little" out, implying they'd been dating weeks or months rather than days.

"We've kept it quiet." Well, he didn't have anyone to tell. The friends he'd made at the gym were more interested in his football statistics than his love life.

"I didn't know you had a boyfriend." Kyla looked at him through narrowed eyes.

"Don't tell anyone," Tabitha said. "Especially not Rhonda. We want it to be a surprise."

Something about Kyla told him she would not be able to keep their news to herself. She'd be delighted to be the first to know anything, good or bad. Especially bad.

"Oh, of course not. You can trust me." Kyla tapped the side of her nose. "Anyway, must go and mingle. You know how it is." She turned and left.

"I don't like her attitude." Logan shook his head as Kyla disappeared down the bleachers. "It's like she thinks she's better than you because she's got a ring on her finger. What's her problem?"

"She's never liked me. Not when we were in school, and not now."

"But she's got to be at least five years older than you. When were you in school together? Grade school?"

"She was a senior in my freshman year at high school. It was a small school, so we had a couple of classes together. Maybe she resented that."

"'Don't tell Rhonda.'" Logan asked. "What did you mean?"

"Kyla can't keep a secret to save herself," Tabitha said. "Especially if she knows it's supposed to be a secret. If you want everyone to know anything in Trinity, you telephone, telegraph, or tell-a-Kyla."

"Ouch." Logan paused to consider the implications of Tabby's words. "Wait a minute. You told Kyla we're dating."

"Yeeesss." She strung the word out like a guilty child admitting she'd eaten the last cookie.

"And you told her to keep it a secret."

"Yes." Tabby sounded more than a little pleased with herself.

"Doesn't that mean everyone in town will know before the ref blows the final whistle?"

"Only half the town." Tabby said in a faux-innocent tone as she flicked her long hair in a way that could only be described as flirtatious. "The other half will find out at church tomorrow morning."

"Does this mean we are officially dating? Like, in a relationship?" Logan mentally crossed his fingers, his toes, and anything else he could cross.

"I guess so." Tabby swung their joined hands, turned to face him, and clasped his other hand.

"Then we should seal it with a kiss." And he did.

———

AFTER THE GAME, Logan headed to Joe's Diner to meet Trent, who'd appeared without any warning that morning, saying he'd been co-opted into playing for the American side. Tabby had headed home, promising she'd relax and read the next book club selection.

Logan ordered himself a soft drink and took a seat at a table in the corner to wait for Trent. The diner was almost empty now because it was early, but he figured it would soon fill up.

"Mind if I join you?" Trent said as he approached the table.

Logan motioned for him to take a seat. "Sorry about the game."

"First time we've lost since I've been old enough to play." Trent fell silent. He had a look about him, the look that said he wanted to raise an awkward topic but didn't know where to start.

Logan stayed silent, a lesson he'd learned from Albert Thomas.

"What are your intentions toward my sister, Logan Wylde?"

Exactly the question he'd been expecting. "Haven't we had this conversation before?" Logan tried to inject a note of humor into his words.

"You might have gone out with Tiffy, but you never had a relationship."

"She was too tied up with her studies. And I was never really interested in her." Especially not since he'd met Tabitha.

"But Tabby . . ." Trent lifted his hands in a tell-me-more gesture. Or maybe it was a come-and-get-me gesture, as though he wanted to start a fight.

"I like her. I've always liked her."

"Kyla says you two have been dating for months."

"Kyla is wrong."

"But you're interested in Tabby?"

"We've been out a couple of times." Logan took a swig of his Bundaberg. Bundaberg ginger beer. Lite. In the bottle. Not as good as Sweet As, the sugar-free version of his all-time favorite soft drink, Lemon and Paeroa, better known as L&P. But Bundaberg ginger beer was a close second, and the last thing he'd expected to find in a small-town American diner.

"Is this a fling or something serious?" Trent picked up a coaster and tapped it on the table. Turn, tap, turn, tap. "Because I warned you about dating my sister."

"You didn't seem to have a problem with me dating Tiffany—"

"I knew you and Tiffany weren't right for each other, and I was right. Look how long that 'relationship' lasted—less than one date."

"Thanks for the vote of confidence." Sure, Logan hadn't been interested in Tiffany. He hadn't known her well enough to be interested and the feeling had been mutual, but that was the purpose of dating. To find out if someone was interesting and interested.

Now, Tabitha was interesting. And he was interested. If the truth be told, he'd been interested from the first time they'd met.

"So why did you warn me off Tabitha that first time you invited me back to Trinity Lakes for Thanksgiving?"

"Her high school boyfriend had just dumped her. She didn't need a rebound relationship."

"And after that?"

"You were headed for the NFL. I knew if Tabby fell for you and you got into the NFL, she'd be left behind. There was no way Dad was going to let her follow you around the country as you played. Not that she'd have wanted to. She's happy in Trinity Lakes. She doesn't want to leave, to travel."

She said she wanted to leave, to travel, although Logan had his doubts. Either way, it wasn't Logan's place to tell Trent what he did and didn't know about his sister.

"My intentions toward your sister are entirely honorable. Always have been."

"So you're serious?"

"I'd like it to be." Logan took a swig of ginger beer. "But I can't speak for Tabitha."

"Aren't you leaving?"

"I've signed up for two months at summer camp, and then I'm supposed to be heading to Europe for three months." Although the European gig could replace him without too much difficulty.

"Does Tabby know?"

"About summer camp? Yes." About Europe? She knew he hadn't planned to stay in Trinity. Of course, plans could change.

"Would you stay if she asked?"

"Stay here? In Trinity? Maybe. But Tabitha wants to travel. We could travel together." He could get her a spot on his European gig. They could sit outside, under the European stars, sampling genuine Italian pizza and pasta with their tour group.

"Tabby has never mentioned anything about wanting to travel."

"Maybe not to you." That came out a little more rudely than

Logan had intended.

"Wha—"

"Hey." Logan raised both hands in a gesture of surrender. "I'm just saying your sister has been running the inn almost single-handed for the past four years and you had no idea about that. It's more than possible there are other things you don't know about her." Like why she had a bedroom wall full of postcards of foreign places.

"I don't think Tabby should leave Trinity Lakes to go traveling. She's not like you. What about the inn and the boat shed?"

"I'm sure she can hire someone to run the inn. And it could be months before the city makes a decision about the boat shed zoning."

"Isn't it time you gave up the whole adventuring lifestyle and settled down? You could live here, and help Tabby run the inn and do whatever she decides to do with the boat shed." Trent pushed away from the table and stood.

"There's Jackson Reilly. I wanted to talk to him. Catch you later, Logan. Trent strode across the room towards Jasper Cohen and a tall man in a cowboy hat.

Was it time to find a regular job, live in a regular house, and have a regular life? If so, should he settle here in Trinity, or somewhere else?

That was his dilemma, what he'd planned to pray about while walking the Camino. But he wasn't walking the Camino. He was here, in Trinity Lakes. He'd prayed, but either God hadn't answered, or Logan had missed the memo.

Logan pushed back his chair, rested his elbows on the table, leaned his chin on his hands, and closed his eyes.

Lord, please guide me. You promised that if I trust You, then You will make my path straight. Right now, it seems anything but straight. It's all twists and turns, like a maze, and I can't see which path You want me to take. Please show me the way—for me and for Tabitha. Amen.

CHAPTER SEVENTEEN

The two months since Logan arrived had sped by. Two months in which Logan and Tabitha had cleaned out her grandmother's rooms, researched the boat shed, and shared fifty-six evenings on the veranda, talking and kissing and cuddling. And falling in love. At least, Logan loved Tabitha. And now it was only four days before Logan left Tabitha, left the Lakeview Inn, and headed to summer camp.

Four days.

Logan was counting down the days, not because he wanted to leave, but because he wanted to stay.

With Tabitha. Forever and always.

Which was ridiculous, because he had no idea what he'd do if he stayed in Trinity Lakes. What paying jobs used his dubious set of skills—he was good at football and talking to teenage boys, and he'd lived in more countries than most people visited in a lifetime.

Four days.

In four days, he'd be off to summer camp. In ten weeks, he'd be off to Europe. Then New Zealand for Christmas and his grandad's eightieth birthday. Then . . . who knew. Something would come up. It always did.

God, I'm trusting You have this all under control, that the right opportunity will present itself, and I'll know it's the right opportunity and accept.

For now, he was off to the gym again. He needed to keep building strength in his ankle. And he needed some ideas for a final romantic before-camp date.

Logan entered the gym and took a seat on a spare stationary cycle. He preferred the treadmill, but his ankle wasn't strong enough to run. Not yet. But he was wearing regular shoes, and his ankle didn't need strapping.

The usual Friday afternoon crowd were here—Brandon, Josh, Justin. No Caleb tonight. Maybe he was out with Kyla. Joel, Hannah's boyfriend, occasionally turned up, but he generally trained on the lake with Hannah.

Logan started with a warm-up on the stationary cycle. Brandon was on the cycle to his left, and Josh to his right.

"You've both lived here forever, right?" Logan asked.

"Me? Yeah," Brandon said. "Why?"

"I need advice. Local knowledge. Where's a good restaurant to go on a date?"

"Depends," Josh said. "What kind of date?"

"Jackson Reilly and Jasper Cohen say Joe's Diner has the best food around," Brandon said.

"I've been there." Logan recalled his conversation with Trent after the Anzac game. "The food is fine, but I was hoping for something more fancy." Something that served coffee by the cup, not the carafe.

"If you want fancy, then dinner at the country club is as fancy as it gets in Trinity." Brandon stopped cycling and leaned back on the bike, stretching his arms above his head.

"I prefer somewhere with bigger portions and smaller prices," Josh said.

"I was hoping for less formal than the country club." Tiffany was a country club kind of woman. Tabitha was not. "And I prefer proper portions."

"If you're looking for good food and good value, then you can't go past Bella Italia on Main Street." Josh climbed off his cycle and slapped Logan on the back. "Good Italian food. Lots of choices—salad, pizza, pasta, meat—and reasonable prices."

"It's kind of casual," Brandon said. "You know, red check tablecloths and Formica chairs. Good food. Authentic. But not so good if you're trying to impress someone."

That sounded like the voice of unpleasant experience. "So no ambience?"

"Ambience?" Brandon raised an eyebrow.

"Atmosphere, stupid." Josh swatted his towel toward Brandon. "He's asking if it's romantic."

"It's not candles and soft music and linen tablecloths, if that's what you're asking."

"They have candles at night. And the radio is usually on," Josh said.

"Is there any place in Trinity Lakes that is candles and soft music and linen tablecloths?" Logan dared to ask.

"You want to ask someone rich, like Liam Darcy. Not poor, dateless losers like us." Brandon gave a vague wave in Josh's direction.

"Speak for yourself." Josh waved back.

"Sorry, Romeo. Remind me—when did you last have a date? A real, meaningful date with someone you actually like?" Brandon turned back toward Logan. "Ignore him. Bella Italia is what you're looking for."

"Sounds like my best option. I'm off to camp on Monday, and I wanted to take Tabitha out for one final dinner before I leave."

"Then take her to Bella Italia." Brandon sounded like the

voice of experience, even if his banter with Josh suggested he had none.

"If you wanted something romantic, you'd figure out how to turn that boat shed in front of the inn into a restaurant." Josh dismounted the bicycle and draped his towel around his neck. "Sunset water views and all that."

"Funny you should say that." Logan stopped pedaling.

"We heard rumors." Josh leaned against the wall, stretching out his calves.

"Rumors? From who?" Logan asked.

"Who do you think?" Josh switched legs. "Kyla."

"Kyla seems to know everything about everyone."

"Everyone except Caleb." Josh and Brandon shared a look that reminded Logan of Pippin and Merry in *Lord of the Rings*.

"What?" Kyla was going to be a camp counselor. If there was trouble in paradise . . . "Wait. I don't want to know."

"Kyla says Tabby has plans to renovate the boat shed and turn it into a Kyla-approved wedding venue." Josh lifted an ankle to stretch out his quad, one hand against the wall for balance. "By November, because that's when she's marrying Caleb."

"Or so she says." Brandon's expression said he was not a member of the Kyla fan club. "Because rumor also says Caleb knows nothing about a November wedding."

"Never mind Kyla." Josh swatted Brandon away. "Logan, tell us what you know about the boat shed."

"The Thomases have submitted paperwork to the council to request the land be rezoned. If the rezoning is approved, then they'll have to request permits. Then find contractors." Logan ticked the tasks off on his fingers.

"That's going to take a while," Brandon said.

"You'll need more than one miracle to get all that done by November." Josh switched legs again.

"Yeah, but . . ." Logan had an idea. "Any chance you two would be interested in doing me a favor?"

They looked at each other in that slightly scary Merry and Pippin way.

"Sure," Josh said.

"What do you want?" Brandon asked.

"Like I said, I'm about to head off to camp." Just as he and Tabitha were getting serious. "I'd like to do something special when I get back, and you've given me an idea . . ."

CHAPTER EIGHTEEN

Tabby took her seat at the cozy candlelit corner table in Bella Italia and placed the red checked cotton napkin across her lap. "I haven't been here since Gran died." Before Logan arrived, she hadn't been anywhere other than church, work, and book club in longer than she cared to remember. Admitting that might make her sound more antisocial than Logan probably thought she was.

It was Logan's last night in Trinity Lakes before he left to head off to summer camp . . . the official reason he'd come to Trinity Lakes in the first place. Sure, summer camp was only fifteen miles south of Trinity Lakes, but it might have well been fifteen million given they'd lived fifteen feet apart for the last two months. And Tabby knew from her own stint at summer camp that being a counselor was full-on, with sixteen-hour days the norm when the campers were on site.

Trinity Lakes didn't have a lot of dining options, so it wasn't entirely a surprise that Logan had chosen Bella Italia for dinner tonight. Although Tabby hadn't visited in a while, she'd always enjoyed their authentic Italian recipes.

"Something smells delicious." She'd always had a fondness for garlic, a fondness Logan fortunately shared.

"I hope so," Logan said. "I wanted to give you a night off from cooking. You're a great cook, but you never get a break."

"I enjoy cooking, but it's good to eat out occasionally." She always appreciated the opportunity to sample someone else's food, to see what combinations of ingredients, herbs, and spices they used, and consider how she could use them to create or improve her own recipes.

A familiar teenager approached. "Hi, my name's Shelby, and I'll be your server tonight." She offered them each a menu.

"Thanks, Shelby." Tabby took the menu. At one time, she'd known it by heart. "Nice to see you again. How long have you been working here?"

"This is my second week." Shelby smoothed the front of her white uniform apron. "I've got all my credits for graduation, so I figured I should earn some spending money for college."

"Good for you," Logan said. "What are you planning to study?"

"I want to get my teaching credentials. I'd love to teach grade school." A customer signaled Shelby from across the room. "Excuse me. I'll be back in a few minutes to get your order."

"No hurry." Tabby lifted her menu and flicked to the list of entrées. Logan did the same, and they agreed to share an antipasto platter and chose an entrée each.

"How do you know the server?" Logan asked.

"Tiffy and I used to babysit Shelby and her younger sisters when we were in high school. And now they're almost adults." It was a sobering thought. Shelby Short was going to college, getting out of Trinity Lakes, getting on with life.

Yet Tabby Thomas was still living in the same town, the same house, the same bedroom she'd lived in her whole life.

"It's a big step," Logan said. "So why didn't you go to college?"

"I didn't go the year Tiffy and Trent went because I got mono over the summer break. It took months to recover enough to consider college—too late to enroll even for the final semester. Then Gran broke her leg, so I looked after Gran and helped run the inn. It was a while before she could manage the stairs, so she did the cooking, and I did the cleaning—all the running up and down the stairs."

"Are you ready to order?" Shelby appeared at Logan's side, pen and paper in hand. Tabby was grateful for the interruption. While she'd told this part of the story often enough over the years, the last part—the part where Gran died—was still a fresh wound.

"Yes, thank you. We'd like to share the antipasto platter for a starter, please, and I'd like chicken parmy for my main." Logan closed his menu and handed it to Shelby. "And Bundaberg ginger beer, please. I like some good Aussie tucker, even if I am a Kiwi."

"Chicken . . . what did you say?" Shelby asked Logan.

"Chicken parmy—chicken parmesan. The Aussies call it chicken parmigiana, or parmy for short."

"Antipasto, chicken parmesan, and a Bundaberg. Got it." Shelby wrote Logan's order on her pad. "And for you, Tabby?"

"I'll have the chicken and mushroom ravioli with lemonade, please."

"No problem. I'll be right back with your drinks." Shelby turned and headed toward the kitchen.

"Now, what were we talking about?" Tabby asked.

"You said you helped your grandmother run the inn after she broke her leg. That sounds painful, especially for someone of her age."

"It was. It seemed to take forever for her to recover. Then she was diagnosed with cancer, and I knew I couldn't leave her." Tabby blinked back unbidden tears, wiping the corner of her eye with her napkin so it wouldn't smudge her mascara. "I'm glad I stayed." As difficult as the last year had been, Tabby wouldn't have given up her time with Gran for anything.

"Tabitha, the responsible one. That's how Trent described you."

She'd always been the responsible one. Not that she wanted to admit that—it sounded boring. Staid. Unattractive. She took a deep breath.

"So was your grandmother why you didn't go to college?"

"Partly Gran, and partly that I didn't know what I wanted to study. Trent has wanted to be a lawyer since he lost his first argument with me and Tiffy."

"He has always been good at arguing his case."

"Tiffy has wanted to be a doctor for as long as I can remember. Perhaps since that day at the lake. I didn't want anything big. I was happy to stay here and help Gran with the B&B."

"Did you ever think about changing your mind and going?"

"Trent and Tiffy both had so many stories about college. I sometimes feel like I missed out on all the fun." It didn't bother her so much now—Tiffy was so busy with her studies that she never seemed to have time for anything anymore, and Trent seemed to spend all his spare time on his intern role.

And she had Logan.

For this evening, at least. He would leave in the morning.

"One Bundaberg and one lemonade." Shelby served the drinks, then reappeared with their antipasto platter, side plates and extra knives.

"Shall I give thanks?" Logan asked. He reached across the table, took her hand, and said grace. At least, she assumed he said grace. Her attention was more focused on the feel of her hand in his, on the rhythm of his words, on the way the candle-light brought out the highlights in his hair. *Sorry, God. Amen.*

"Amen."

They talked about Tiffy and Trent and college and high school as they nibbled on parma ham, salami, olives, and various cheeses. It seemed like only a few minutes passed before Shelby reappeared with their main dishes, but it must have been at least half an hour.

"One 'chicken parmy' for the gentleman, and creamy ravioli for the lady." Shelby placed their meals on the table.

"Thank you," Tabby said. "It smells delicious."

"Enjoy your meals." Shelby turned on her heel and headed to the next table.

Logan picked up his fork and knife and sliced into his cheese-covered chicken. "I meant to ask earlier, what was that official-looking envelope you got in the mail today? Was it from the council?"

No, not from the council. The envelope had contained her brand-new first-ever passport, which she'd impulsively applied for after she and Logan had talked about the postcards in her room and before she'd found out about Gran's boat shed dreams.

"That would have been too much to hope for." Tabitha took a mouthful of creamy chicken pasta. It was as delicious as she remembered.

"If the council had been able to review the zoning this quickly, the answer would probably have been no."

"True. I guess we'll have to wait."

"So what was in the envelope?"

Should she tell him? Logan had seen her bedroom, her postcard collection. He knew about her dreams of travel. Knew there were days when she wanted nothing more than to throw everything in—work, church, the inn—and go traveling. Like Logan. To have no cares beyond the next place, the next thrill, the next adventure.

But her dreams had been just that for so long—dreams.

She'd dream, then her sensible side, her responsible side, would kick in and remind her why such a dream was impossible and immature and irresponsible. She was tied to Trinity Lakes by Gran. By the inn. By the rowing club.

Or was she? Grannie Gracie would say that was the decision she had to make.

Did she play it safe? Did she stay as she was, Tabby the responsible homebody?

Or should she be a more adventurous Tabby, a Tabby who was prepared to take a risk? Adventurous Tabby would tell Logan about the passport.

"I applied for my passport a few weeks ago. It arrived." Her first-ever passport, green and pristine, with United States of America on the outside and her name and photograph on the inside.

"You got it renewed?" Of course Logan would assume she'd had a passport before. He'd probably had one since he was born.

"It's my first." She tried to keep the pride from her voice, because a world traveler like Logan wouldn't think it was any kind of big deal.

"Wow." Logan actually sounded impressed, to his credit. "Congratulations. Does this mean you're planning to travel somewhere soon?"

"No plans. Not yet." And possibly not ever if they got the green light for the boat shed renovations.

"I could suggest some plans." Logan reached across the table and took her hand, caressing her ring finger as he spoke. "My grandad turns eighty in December. We're planning a big family reunion for his birthday and Christmas. You could come with me—you'd enjoy summer in New Zealand. We could visit Hobbiton and the Waitomo Caves. I saw those postcards on your wall." His words came out in almost a single breath.

"Wait a minute." Tabby pulled away and raised her right

hand in a "stop" gesture. "I'm not going anywhere." And she certainly wasn't gallivanting around the globe with Logan. Not without a ring on her finger.

"But you applied for a passport. Surely you want to go somewhere. What about all those postcards on your wall?"

"I applied before we found out about Gran's dream to renovate the boat shed. Now I want to stay in Trinity and work on that."

"So that's your dream?"

"It was Gran's dream. I want to do it in her memory." Hadn't they had this conversation a dozen times already?

"But do you want to do it for yourself? Is renovating the boat shed what you want to do? Is it God's plan for your life?"

"I believe I'm exactly where God wants me." That was Tabby's honest truth. "I was disappointed I couldn't go to college at first, but after Gran got sick, I realized my mono had kept me home to care for her. It was God working out His plan in my life."

"Even now she's gone?"

Tabby took a breath to answer, but Logan went on.

"I can believe God wanted you here to support your gran through her illness and to help with the inn, but I'm not convinced you're meant to run the inn forever. Especially not if you also want to travel and to turn the boat shed into an event venue. And I don't think that's what your grandmother would have wanted for you."

Something about his tone lit a fire inside her.

"You have no idea what Gran would have wanted. You didn't know her like I did," she said in a hissing whisper, loud enough to show her anger but soft enough that they shouldn't be overheard.

"And you're so busy helping Hannah achieve her dream and chasing your Gran's dream that you never take even a minute to consider what your own dream might be. What God's plan for you might be."

"Are you seriously trying to tell me God's plan for my life?" She'd never picked Logan as a patriarchal type or a mansplainer.

"You say you believe you're exactly where God wants you. I don't."

"If you don't believe you're where God wants you, perhaps you should do something about that." Perhaps God meant for Logan to stay here. In Trinity Lakes. With Tabby.

"Sure, I'm a little fuzzy on the details about my future, but I do believe God brought me to Trinity and that He wants me at summer camp. Beyond that, I'm open." He shrugged, as if not knowing what he wanted to do with his life wasn't a problem. "But that wasn't what I meant. I meant that I don't think you're where God wants you."

"What?" Anger swelled up inside at his unfair accusation.

"Me not knowing God's plan for your life isn't a problem. You not knowing God's plan . . . now, that's a problem." He reached across the table and took her hand. "It seems to me that you're spending all your time on other people's dreams and plans. There's no time left over for your own."

"I have no idea what you mean." She pulled away from Logan's hold and clasped both her hands in her lap.

"So what about coming to New Zealand with me for Christmas? Wait a second . . . I'm going to Europe after I finish at summer camp. We could go together. Start in Paris, finish in Rome."

Paris? Rome? The two cities she'd said she'd most like to visit.

Wait.

What kind of a person did he think she was?

"I'm not gallivanting around the globe with a boyfriend." Tabby's words came out as a vicious whisper.

"Not just 'a boyfriend.' Me." Logan looked at her with that puppy-dog look she'd once found irresistible. But not tonight.

"Is traveling and working and never having a regular job God's plan for your life? I don't think so."

But what if that was God's plan for Logan's life? Could she—sensible, responsible Tabby—share that lifestyle? Or was this mess of a conversation God telling her to back off?

"Maybe we can find out together," Logan said. "Because there's nothing I'd like more than exploring the world and living life with you by my side. Forever and always. Wherever God leads us."

Tabby sat upright in her chair, resisting the temptation to fold her arms like a sulky schoolgirl at his outrageous suggestion. "But suggesting I go to Europe with you. That's . . . not appropriate."

"There's nothing inappropriate. The problem is you still don't trust me. Part of you still believes Trent's tall tales, that I'm wild Logan Wylde, a womanizing party animal."

"I—"

"Can I interest you in dessert?" Shelby approached their table with a nervous smile and the dessert menu in hand.

Logan turned to take the menus. "Tha—"

"I'm good, thank you," Tabby said. "Can we get the check, please?" She wanted to get out of here, to get back to her room, and cry. She'd thought their relationship was going so well, but tonight's conversation had her second, third, and fourth guessing herself.

She'd thought they were on the same page. Now she wasn't even sure they were reading the same book. Was she seeking and following God's plan for her life, as she believed . . . or was what she saw as service merely fulfilling other people's dreams?

Or was Logan wrong? After all, Logan's faith seemed to be all about himself and his dreams and travels.

Where was his sense of responsibility? Where was his

understanding of the importance of family and friends and a local Christian community? Jesus's command to love our neighbor meant helping those in need, as demonstrated by the biblical Martha, and by her own dear Gran.

Gran had raised her to believe in service before self. Did Logan share that belief?

CHAPTER NINETEEN

By eight o'clock on Monday morning, Logan had packed his bag, loaded the panniers on his motorbike, and said what he hoped were temporary goodbyes to Tabitha and to Albert Thomas. Albert, predictably, had said Logan was welcome to stay any time.

Tabitha hadn't. She hadn't said a word on their way home from the restaurant last night. She'd disappeared into her room as soon as they arrived back at the inn and avoided him this morning. Not that he could blame her, after their last conversation. So much for not letting the sun go down on their anger. And now he was off to summer camp for two months, with no opportunity to make things right.

He had no idea what he'd said wrong, but he would have plenty of time to think about it—his next few weeks were going to be pretty full-on at camp, and he wasn't going to have time to come back into town and make up with her.

He'd been hanging out, waiting for summer camp when he first arrived. But now that it was time to leave Trinity Lakes and the Lakeview Inn and Tabitha, he didn't want to go. With one final glance at the inn, Logan revved his motorbike and headed south.

The feeling of not wanting to go wasn't new. He'd had the same feeling the day before he'd been due to fly from Singapore to Auckland to head to boarding school for the first time. He'd had the same feeling the first time he boarded a plane from London to Seattle to head to college. He'd even had the same feeling when he'd boarded the flight from Seattle to head south for what would become his short-lived football career.

But all those times, the feeling of loss had been tempered by the knowledge that he was growing up and moving on to life's next big adventure—to high school, to college, and into the work-force. Not that most people considered pro football to be work.

He rode over the bridge. Now he was out of town, he could open up the throttle on his motorbike. Camp Trinity wasn't far out of town, but it was far enough to build up some speed.

Leaving this time was different. This time he wasn't heading off on life's next big adventure. This time, he felt more like he was leaving life behind.

Life with Tabitha. Life in a family. Life in a small town where everyone knew everyone else, and where everyone cared. A community.

He was going to miss Tabitha. Miss seeing her at breakfast. Miss helping her clear out Gran's suite. Miss talking with her in the evenings. Miss having her always by his side.

Would she miss him? She'd miss his help—he hoped. She'd be working more hours at the rowing club now the days were getting longer, but she'd have no less work to do at the inn. If anything, she'd have more.

Sure, Logan wanted Tabitha to miss him. But he didn't want her to bury herself in her workaholic ways, doing everything herself and not asking for or accepting help.

But he couldn't stay. He'd committed to these ten weeks at

summer camp, and he was a man of his word. It was too late to pull out now, especially as he'd heard they were already down one leader after Caleb's sister somehow managed to fall off a roof and break a leg.

It was too late to pull out of summer camp, but maybe he should reconsider the rest of his year. The thought of jumping on yet another plane for yet another long-haul flight didn't hold the promise of adventure it had held at thirteen or eighteen or even twenty-two.

Now he wanted to stay.

He reached the turnoff for the camp. Now it was time to adjust his attitude. There was going to be enough attitude already with a camp full of teens. No one needed his as well. He was here to lead a bunch of teens and do everything he could to ensure they all had a great camp experience.

And that meant turning his attention to camp and the teens he would lead.

———

"Tabitha Thomas, what is wrong with you?" Hannah's Granny Gracie stood in the doorway of the rowing club, hands on hips and eyes like daggers. She didn't stamp her foot, but she might as well have.

"I beg your pardon?"

"Your grandmother charged me with her dying breath to treat you as one of my own, and God help me if I fail in my final assignment."

Okay, now Tabby was worried. "What's the problem?"

"I popped into First National Bank to have a little chat with that nice Mille Avery about my account, but she was busy with that good-looking cowboy. What's his name?" Her tone wasn't quite so shrill.

"Liam Darcy?" Tabby had spotted his truck speeding past her as she'd walked to work.

"No, the other one. The neighbor. The one with the brothers."

"Do you mean the Reillys? Jackson Reilly?" Was Gracie ever going to get to the point?

"That's the one. He was at the bank, and looking rather worried if you ask me. Anyway, I ran into Rhonda Ingalls while I was waiting, and she said"—the shrill tone was back—"'That handsome Logan Wylde isn't staying at the inn anymore.'"

"He's volunteering at Camp Trinity—"

Gracie lifted her hand in a "stop" signal. "I hadn't finished. Rhonda told me you and Logan had an argument, and he's left town. And now you have the sheriff's daughter staying with you after she had an argument with her father."

"You know Rhonda doesn't always get the details right." And sometimes she got them dead wrong, like when she'd practically tripped over Leah and Marcus on their fake date.

"So Logan is still staying at the inn with you?"

"Like I said, he's volunteering at Camp Trinity—which is why he came to Trinity Lakes in the first place."

"So you didn't have an argument with him?

"I wouldn't call it an argument. I'd call it more like a minor disagreement." And the Grand Canyon was a small hole in the ground.

"That was not what I heard." She sniffed. "Rhonda said you two were fighting like fishwives in Bella Italia the other night."

Tabby's shoulders dropped as all the fight went out of her.

"So maybe it was more than a disagreement. What did Rhonda tell you?"

"She didn't repeat the whole conversation—you know how discreet she is."

As discreet as wearing scarlet to a funeral.

"She said it sounded like you and that nice Logan Wylde had

broken up, and it was my job to find out why and get you back together. After all, I promised your dear grandmother I'd look out for you. So here I am." Granny Gracie folded her arms with a huff that said she'd been assigned a task, and she was going to complete the task whether she liked it or not.

"I suppose I should be grateful Rhonda sent you rather than coming herself."

"Indeed you should. Now, I baked some cookies this morning, so let's have a nice glass of iced tea and a cookie and you can tell me all about it." Gracie ushered Tabby toward the iced tea and the cookie jar, then outside where they could sit on one of the benches without being overheard, but where Tabby could still see the door in case any customers arrived.

Once they were seated, Gracie spoke again, more quietly this time.

"Correct me if I've got this wrong, but Rhonda said you and Logan were fighting about going somewhere together. Or not going. Rhonda wasn't clear."

"Logan asked me if I'd like to go to France and Italy with him in the fall, then to New Zealand to see his family at Christmas."

"France and Italy? Sounds romantic. And a trip to New Zealand? That sounds wonderful. And serious—inviting you to meet his family."

"But we're not married. We're not even engaged—"

"If you said yes to visiting his family, you might find you were engaged." Gracie peered at Tabby over the top of her glasses.

Tabby blinked long and slow so Gracie wouldn't notice that she was rolling her eyes. There were some days when she could see exactly where Hannah's mother had inherited her flair for the dramatic—from her own mother, Granny Gracie.

"Don't you roll your eyes at me, young lady. I'm not stupid. A summer fling doesn't invite you halfway around the world to meet his family. That's him telling you he's serious."

"But alone? Just me and Logan? What kind of Christian witness is that?"

"Pish posh. You're making excuses. Rhonda and I have both known you since you were a baby. We know your father and your grandmother—God rest her precious soul—raised you properly. We know you'd never do anything inappropriate or irresponsible."

"Which is why I can't go traveling with him in Europe."

"He's a good Christian boy. Young man. Whatever. I have to wonder if you've misunderstood him."

You want to travel, don't you? Why don't you come with me to Europe? You'll love it—Paris in the summer, Italy in the fall. Then come back to New Zealand with me for Christmas.

She hadn't misunderstood.

Had she?

"What exactly did he say?"

Tabby repeated his words as best she could remember them.

"This trip to Europe—was that a holiday, or did he have a job?"

"A—" She'd assumed he was heading to Europe for a job right up until he invited her to join him. Then she'd figured it must be an extended holiday, because how could Logan offer her a job? "I don't know."

"Did you ask?"

"I assumed—"

"You know what they say about assumptions. Why didn't you ask instead of assuming? Don't you know him better than that?"

She'd thought she had . . .

"You assumed the worst. You doubt Logan. His intentions. I can see it in your face. Why?"

"Trent had all these stories about the wild things Logan got up to at college—"

"Your brother is a typical youngest child." She held up a

hand. "Yes, I know. He's only younger by half an hour. But just like you've always been the oldest, the responsible one, he's always been the youngest. The reckless one. The one who does whatever he wants and doesn't think of the consequences."

Granny Gracie wasn't wrong.

"That's partly your fault, of course. Yours and Tiffany's." Granny Gracie made a shoo-shoo gesture as though she could shoo away Tabby's problems as easily as a fly.

What?

"You two were always there to fix his mistakes when he did something wrong or stupid. I know you both meant well, but Trent has unfortunately learned that he doesn't have to fix up his own mistakes, because someone else will do it for him. Usually you. Sometimes Tiffany."

As usual, Granny Gracie was right. "How do you know all this?"

"Your grandmother and I met each week to pray for our grandchildren—hers and mine."

"I knew you met every week. I didn't realize you were prayer partners." And if she knew anything at all about Granny Gracie, she was still praying for them all.

"We were. And that's why there's not a lot I don't know about your family. I certainly know that your brother has never learned to take responsibility for his actions. And that will be his undoing one day, mark my words."

"But what about Logan? How are you so sure he's a Christian, that his intentions are honorable?"

"Because your grandmother told me, of course. And because I've done my research. Haven't you seen his Twitter profile?"

"Logan has a Twitter profile?" Grannie Gracie was on Twitter?

"He hasn't updated it in half of forever—I've checked—but he has Proverbs 3:5–6 in his profile."

"'Trust in the Lord with all of your heart.'"

"Your grandmother was always impressed with Logan, from the first time he visited your house. She always knew he was a strong Christian. She assumed you knew as well."

"I didn't know. Trent implied he wasn't, and—"

"You believed your brother. I understand that, and now you know what I think of your brother. But now it's time to believe Logan, and to look inside your own heart, and to not let the sun go down on your anger." She waved a hand. "I know, I know. It's a bit late for that. So now you have to figure out how to make it right before Logan leaves. Before you miss out on whatever God has for the two of you."

Granny Gracie was right, but only half right. What about Logan's accusation that Tabby was too busy working and wasn't seeking God's plan for her life?

CHAPTER TWENTY

I t didn't take long for Logan to settle into the routine of camp and the role of camp counselor. Come to think of it, summer camp wasn't a lot different from his teenage years at boarding school and the many school camps he'd attended, first as a schoolboy camper and later as a peer mentor. The only difference was that he'd spent five years living and attending school with the friends he'd made at that first week-long school camp. They'd done all the usual getting-to-know-you exercises and team-building activities, and they'd bonded over the shared experiences of ice-cold showers and lukewarm food.

And now he was the one in charge, the counselor charged with motivating and sometimes coercing his group to step out of their comfort zones and try something new.

Today they were rock climbing on a real rock face. They'd spent a fair few hours learning the techniques on the relative safety of an indoor wall. Today they got to try the real thing.

Two hours later, everyone had climbed the cliff and abseiled down, and were filled with the triumph of success. The group chattered among themselves as Logan led them into the dining hall. Hard to believe they'd been a group of almost-silent strangers just three days ago.

They all took their seats for dinner while Jonas said grace, then lined up a table at a time for yet another great meal from Chris and Marcus, the Aussie chefs who were producing meals much better than typical camp fare.

"Are you a teacher?" Max asked as Logan took his first mouthful.

"No," Logan said. "Why do you ask?"

"You seem like a teacher."

Logan raised his eyebrows, a silent signal for Max to say more.

"You know how to talk to us. Like we're actual people."

"Not like that Kyla chick," Finlay said through a mouthful of mac and cheese. "She always sounds like she's telling us off."

"Close your mouth when you eat, dude." Logan made a "shut it" gesture toward Finlay. "None of us want to see that."

Finlay chewed and swallowed. "That's what I mean. Kyla would've given me an entire sermon."

"I think the leadership team prefers to call them devotionals." Logan did his best to keep from smiling.

"When Kyla gets going, it's a full-on sermon," Max said. "One of those all-sinners-go-to-hell ones, not the Jesus-loves-you stuff Jonas tells us."

"You realize both can be true, right?" Finlay scooped another fork full of mac and cheese into his mouth, closed it, and ate with an exaggerated chewing motion that was only a little less unpleasant to watch than him talking with his mouth full.

This was when some camp counselors might have chosen to intervene with a relevant Bible verse. Logan preferred to sit back and listen. Lecturing and sermonizing didn't bring teens into the Kingdom, and what worked for one teen wouldn't work for another. Which meant spending time with each teen and getting to know what made them tick.

"You sure you're not a teacher?" Max asked again.

"Like I said, no."

"Shame. You'd be a good teacher."

"Yeah. I wish my teachers were as cool as you." This time, Finlay had managed to swallow before speaking.

"School is different to camp. It's ruled by bells." Max ting-tinged his fork on his glass.

"And tests." Finlay shoved one final forkful into his mouth.

"It's better than home." Jimmie wouldn't meet Logan's eyes.

Logan made a mental note to find out more about Jimmie and his home life.

"We never get to have fun at school. Camp is fun." Finlay dropped his fork onto his empty plate.

"Some teachers make school fun. I bet you'd be one of those teachers." Max pointed to Logan with his knife.

The teens compared notes on schools and teachers until Jonas stood and tapped on his mug, signaling it was time to clear the tables and head outside for their evening program.

The conversation stayed with Logan during the evening's campfire singsong and an inspirational message from one of the camp staff—tonight was Kyla's turn. Her three-point inspirational message was obviously rehearsed because her content was flawless and her delivery was pitch-perfect. No doubt the boys in Logan's cabin would still find a way to misconstrue Kyla's earnest words.

"You're quiet tonight." Jonas appeared at Logan's side. "Thinking about anything in particular?"

"Just something one of the boys in my group said."

Jonas didn't say anything. Like Albert Thomas, Jonas was one of those rare people who didn't mind gaps in a conversation . . . probably because he'd learned that most people didn't like the gaps, so would speak to stop the silence.

"They asked if I was a teacher. Said I'd be a good one, that they wished I taught at their school."

"They're not wrong. You would be a good teacher. You've got the right temperament, and you're good with teens."

"Thank you." Logan hadn't been fishing for a compliment, but he wasn't going to reject the feedback. "Teaching isn't something I've considered."

"Is it something you could do?" Jonas asked.

"I don't have a teaching qualification, if that's what you're asking."

"But you graduated college, right?"

"Yeah."

"What's your major?"

"Geography, with a business minor—accounting and economics."

"You may not know this, but in my spare time, I'm the deputy principal at Trinity Lakes High School. We're always looking for good social science teachers. Mind you, what we really need is a part-time football coach."

Was this guy for real? "I also played college football. Special teams. Too small for defense, but I know my way around a West Coast offense."

"You could be an answer to prayer. If you were interested."

Interested? In a job that kept him in Trinity Lakes, near Tabitha? "I'm interested, but I'll have to pray about it."

"Good answer. You pray about it and let me know." Jonas slapped him on the back. "I'll send you some links on how to get your state teaching credentials. It only takes a year, and you can teach while you're doing the course."

"Thanks. Goodnight." Logan waved as Jonas walked away.

Well, Jonas—and the teens—had certainly given Logan something to think about. And pray about.

Lord, I believe Tabitha is the woman You've chosen for me. But I don't have a job to keep me in Trinity Lakes, and Tabitha doesn't seem keen on leaving. This could be an option. Lord, I know You have a plan for my life, and for Tabitha's life. I ask that You please make my path clear to me, and make Tabitha's clear to her. And Lord, I'd love it if our paths were together. If that's Your will, please make it obvious to both of us.

———

TONIGHT WAS BOOK CLUB NIGHT, and Tabby had invited Hannah and Leah over for dinner first. There was no way she was reneging tonight—after the bust-up with Logan, she needed some girl time. She'd also offered to host the book club meeting tonight, as the café had another event on, and they were expecting a smaller turnout than normal.

As they enjoyed their simple meal together, Hannah pulled out her phone to show a picture of her and Joel on their last date. They made a cute couple.

After they'd finished their meal—and finished teasing Hannah—Tabby rose to clear the table.

Hannah and Leah chatted while Tabby loaded the dishwasher, unloaded a range of cheeses and cold meats from the refrigerator, and arranged them on platters.

"Tabby, do you ever rest?" Leah asked from the counter. "You're always doing something, and it makes me feel lazy. Like I should be helping."

"I get a solid eight hours sleep every night." Tabby couldn't keep the defensive tone from her voice.

"I don't mean sleep. I mean rest. Do you ever just go for a walk and enjoy the beauty around us? Do you ever sit down and read a book for pleasure—"

"I read the book club books." Tonight was supposed to be her opportunity to vent and have her friends offer love and support. Not their opportunity to find fault with her work ethic.

"I think Leah meant something other than a book club book," Hannah said. "Look at you. You're wiping away invisible crumbs."

"It needs to be clean for the guests." Tabby folded the cleaning cloth and positioned it carefully beside the sink at exactly ninety degrees, just as Gran had taught her.

"It's already spotless. Let's go into the lounge and sit down." Leah grabbed Tabby by the elbow and gently manhandled her into the love seat, then sat beside her. "Sit. Stay. Stop cleaning."

"Do you have any idea how much dust there is in an old house like this?" Tabby did not appreciate being treated like a badly behaved pet. "I don't want anyone writing an online review that says the place is dirty."

"They'd need a microscope to find a speck of dust anywhere except perhaps your Gran's suite." Hannah took a seat on the sofa opposite. "And the family area is off-limits to guests anyway."

"I've finished cleaning out Gran's bedroom and bathroom." Which was true, but only because Logan had helped. "Now I'm waiting for Joel and Justin to renovate the bathroom, and Jasper's crew will paint that and the bedroom. Then it will be ready to rent out."

"How are you going on the living room?" Hannah asked.

"I'll finish it as soon as I get a spare moment. You both run your own businesses. You know it takes all your time."

"No, it doesn't," Hannah said.

"It shouldn't," Leah said at the same time.

"What do you mean?" Tabby looked from Hannah to Leah.

"I know the inn is a business, but it shouldn't take all your time. You still need to have a life." Hannah leaned back in her chair.

Easy for Hannah to say. She'd been gifted her business by her mega-rich father. That wasn't to say Hannah was incapable or lazy or entitled. She was smart and hardworking and down-to-earth. But she'd had an easier time of starting her business than Leah.

"I agree," Leah said. "I'm at the shop by seven in the morning six days a week, but I close by four on weekdays, and at midday on Saturday. I never work more than fifty hours a week—less now I can afford hired help a few days a week."

"And I couldn't run the rowing club without you and Lawrence covering the afternoon and weekend shifts."

Well, good for you two, Tabby wanted to say. But she didn't. Running a store or a rowing club wasn't like running a B&B. Someone needed to cook breakfast, set the table, clean up, then clean the rooms and wash the sheets and towels and . . . the list went on. Hannah and Leah could lock up and leave work behind. Tabby couldn't.

"Even if I have to do some ordering or admin on Saturday afternoon, I make sure to take my Sabbath rest on Sunday." Leah looked Tabby in the eye.

"And I take two full days off every week," Hannah said. "Tabby, I hadn't thought of it until now, but do you ever take a day off? You have guests every day of the week. Please tell me it's not just you."

"Dad—"

"We know your father minds the inn while you're at the rowing club," Leah said. "I think Hannah's asking if you have hired help."

"Tabitha Thomas, have you been working seven days a week since your Gran died and you never told me?" Was Hannah angry or upset? Tabby couldn't tell.

"She didn't tell me, either," Leah added. "You can't spend your whole life working, Tabby. You need rest. It's a biblical principle."

"I didn't invite you two for dinner so you could gang up on me about not resting enough." She'd already had the you-need-to-rest-more lecture.

"I'm sorry, Tabby. We didn't mean to sound like we were hassling you." Leah reached over and patted her arm. "Why did you want to talk to us?"

"Logan and I had a fight, and—"

"What did you fight about?" Leah turned and rested a hand on Tabby's arm.

"When?" Hannah asked. "Why didn't you tell me at work?"

"The night before he left. He asked me if I'd go traveling with him after he's finished at summer camp."

"Traveling? Where?" Leah asked.

"Alone?" Hannah frowned as if thinking. "I mean, just the two of you?"

"Just the two of us, travelling to Rome and Paris. Why would Logan ask something that's so clearly inappropriate?"

"Do you think you might have misunderstood?" Hannah gave her an assessing look.

"You have before." Leah leaned back in the chair.

"When?"

"Tabby, you're my best friend and I love you, so please remember I'm saying this in the spirit of love. Not offense." Hannah leaned forward and rested her elbows on her knees.

"We all read that book Kyla picked for book club, so we all know the difference." Tabby hadn't finished the book—she'd been too busy—but she'd read enough to understand the futility of taking offense.

"Kyla might have picked that book, but I'm not sure she read it." Leah snickered. "If she read the book, she missed the point."

"You told us that Trent told you that Logan wasn't a Christian. Right?" Hannah asked.

"Trent didn't say it in so many words. He implied it."

"Trent implied it, and you believed him despite all the evidence to the contrary." Hannah would make a great lawyer.

"What evidence?"

"Logan goes to Jackson's church." Hannah held up a finger.

"I didn't know Logan went to church." Tabby folded her arms.

"Fair point," Leah said. "You were always working, so you had no idea whether he went to church or not."

"Besides, going to church doesn't make someone a Christian." She could name any number of churchgoers who certainly didn't act like Christians once they'd left the building.

"He's volunteering at a summer camp run by Christians." Hannah held up another two fingers. "Volunteering. For two whole months."

"Camp Trinity isn't a Bible camp, and the counselors don't have to be Christians," Tabby said. "And they're not all volunteers. Some of the specialist staff are paid."

"Then there's all the help he gave you around the inn." Hannah held up another finger and waved in the general direction of the kitchen.

"And there's his jobs—a lot of his jobs have been working with disabled or at-risk teens." Leah said.

"Working with underprivileged teens speaks well to his character." Hannah gave a thoughtful nod.

"How do you know that?" It was news to Tabby.

"I may have looked him up online," Leah said in a faux-innocent tone.

"You cyberstalked my . . ." She wanted to say "my boyfriend," but was he? After their last conversation? Did she even want him to be her boyfriend?

"I checked him out on all Dad's favorite search engines."

"Your dad is the sheriff."

Sherriff Thompson's "favorite search engines" probably weren't available to members of the public.

"Did you know Logan was something called Head Boy at his high school? And that he earned something called the Duke of Edinburgh's Gold Award? You have to do a big community service project for that."

"That doesn't make him a Christian. And if it's all so obvious, why didn't either of you figure out he was a Christian?" Tabby said.

"Because you told us he wasn't, and we believed you. We didn't have all the facts."

"I feel stupid for not figuring it out." If Tabby was a drinker, now would be the time for a glass of something stiff, to stifle how stupid she felt. "And for doubting him."

"You're not stupid. Remind me, how did your dear brother introduce you to Logan?" Hannah's words had the annoying tone of someone who knew they were right.

"Trent said, 'Tabby, meet my roommate. Logan Wylde—Wylde by name, and wild by nature.' Then he—Trent—laughed."

And Logan had offered the uncomfortable smile of someone who had heard the bad joke too often to count, but who was too well-mannered to contradict his host.

"Exactly. With an introduction like that, it's no wonder you expected him to be wild, an adventurer . . . not a Christian."

"Then why did he ask me to go to Europe with him?"

"I don't know, but I can't imagine him suggesting anything inappropriate." Leah leaned over and rubbed Tabby's knee the way a mother might comfort a child. "Are you sure you heard him right? That you haven't misinterpreted him?"

"That's what Granny Gracie said." Tabby rubbed at a small stain on the arm of the chair.

"You talked to Granny Gracie?" Hannah asked. "What did she say?"

Tabby leaned back and rolled her eyes. "She thinks I've got completely the wrong idea and that I need to talk to Logan."

"She's right," Leah said.

"My Granny Gracie is always right. That means you could fix this 'big dilemma' with Logan by talking to him."

"But—"

"Tabby, I know he's at camp, but he's not working 24/7."

Hannah sat back and folded her arms. "There must be some time you can talk to him."

"Have you called him?" Leah asked.

Of course she hadn't. She didn't speak, but Leah would see the answer in her expression.

"Has he called you?"

Tabby didn't answer.

"He has. And you ghosted him." Hannah shook her head, looking exactly like Grandma Gracie before she delivered a lecture. "Really, Tabby. We're not in high school anymore. You need to talk to him."

"I don't think she's told us everything." Leah leaned back and stretched her arms above her head. "I think Logan said something else, something which upset her or made her angry, and that's the real reason she hasn't spoken to him."

"Is this one of your dad's questioning techniques?" Tabby asked. "Putting words in the suspect's mouth?"

"Of course not. My dad would never accuse someone without a reason. He always follows the evidence."

Sure. Like he had with Justin "breaking in" to Olivia Darcy's car.

"I think Leah might be right," Hannah said. "You've been quiet since Logan left, as though you're thinking something over. What did Logan say?" Hannah wore the dog-with-a-bone expression that said she wasn't letting this go. Tabby could either answer quickly or answer slowly, but she would answer.

And she wanted to answer.

"Kind of what you two were saying before. I work too much. I say yes too often. I'm so busy helping other people achieve their dreams that I don't consider my own dreams or pray and seek what God might be calling me to do."

There was a long silence in the room before Leah spoke. "Do you think Logan might be right?"

"He might, but I could ask him the same question. What's his dream? What's his God-given calling? Surely it's not to spend his life gallivanting around the globe, even if he is gallivanting with noble intent."

"Have you asked him?" Leah pointed toward Tabby.

"He said he didn't know, but he's searching."

"That's a good answer." Hannah sat back, considering her words. "The Bible promises that if we seek, we will find."

"Sometimes it takes a little longer than we might want," Leah said. "Like Dad agreeing to me and Justin dating."

"What is your dream?" Hannah asked. "What do you want to do with your life? I know you stayed in Trinity because you needed to help your grandmother look after the inn, but I don't see you spending the rest of your life running a B&B in this tiny town that's nothing more than a dot on a map. It's not you."

"I love living here." Tabby couldn't keep the hurt out of her voice.

"I know you do. I do as well. But there's a whole wide world out there, and I'm not convinced this cute corner is where God wants you." Hannah looked at her with kind eyes. "If you could go anywhere you want, be anyone you want, where would you go? Who would you be? Who is God calling you to be?"

I'd be Tabitha Wylde.

The words leaped into her consciousness like a fish leaping out of the lake.

"Well?" Hannah asked. "I can tell from that look on your face that you have an answer. And it's not being Tabitha Thomas of Trinity Lakes."

"I'd be with Logan. Wherever that was."

"Is that what you want? Or is that your God-given calling?" Leah asked. "Because you know as well as I do that one is more important than the other."

"What about the verse where God promises to give us the desires of our heart?" Tabby asked.

"I can answer that one." A new voice came from the door. A male voice. Dad. "Do you mind if I join you?"

Tabby turned and signaled him in, and he took a seat. "Martha and I often discussed this verse, and we found it works two ways. First, God gives us our desires. If we're following Him, then the desires of our heart are what He desires for us."

"That makes sense," Leah said.

"That's like the quote Gran had on the wall."

"The Augustine quote?" Dad asked. "That was one of her favorites. 'Love God, and do whatever you please: for the soul trained in love to God will do nothing to offend the One who is Beloved.'"

"If we're trusting that God knows best rather than relying on our own understanding, then God's will becomes the desire of our heart." Leah tapped her forefinger against her lips. "Then we get our desire because God gave it to us."

"What does that mean for Tabby and Logan?" Hannah asked. "Or for me and Joel, or Leah and Justin?"

"The same as it means for all of us—if we can trust God's direction and calling for our own lives, we can trust that God will bring us the people and relationships He wants us to have—all kinds of relationships."

"What do you think of Logan? Of Tabby and Logan?" Hannah asked.

"Logan is a fine man. I'd be proud to have him join the family . . . if that's God's will and your desire. Yours and Logan's."

CHAPTER TWENTY-ONE

On Saturday morning, Logan waved goodbye to the last of this week's campers and checked the time on his phone. Eleven. Today was his afternoon off, and he had just enough time to ride up to Trinity Lakes and find Leah before Trinity Organics closed.

Thirty minutes later, he opened the door to Leah's store. Leah was on the phone. She looked up as he entered and signaled for him to wait, a look of surprise on her face. As she wound up the call and replaced the phone on the charger, the surprise morphed into more of an assessing look.

"Hi, Logan. How may I help you?" Leah turned on her best serve-the-customer smile.

"Can we keep this conversation between us?"

"You mean, not tell Tabby?"

Logan gave a quick nod as he met her open gaze.

"I don't like gossip and I don't like secrets." Leah narrowed her eyes as if accusing him of one . . . or both.

"It's not gossip. And it's not a secret. It's a surprise. For Tabitha."

"A good surprise?"

"I hope so."

"Then I can help." She clapped her hands like a five-year-old at a birthday party. "I love surprises."

"I don't know what Tabitha has told you, but we had a bit of a . . ." A what? An argument? A fight? "A misunderstanding."

"That wasn't quite how I heard it." She folded her arms across her chest.

"I messed up. I said something, she misunderstood, and now she's not returning my calls." *Lord, I asked her, and now she's backing away and ghosting me, and I don't know how to fix it. I'm upset and I'm confused.* "I need to do something to make it right."

"A big romantic gesture?" Leah had the demeanor of an ancient schoolmarm.

"I guess so. Just no Romeo-on-the-balcony kind of ideas. I'm no Shakespeare scholar, but even I know that ended badly." Logan frowned and shook his head, as though the movement might alter the memory.

"What about Heath Ledger in *Ten Things I Hate About You?* When he serenades her at soccer practice?"

"I was hoping for something a little less humiliating." Logan put his head in his hands. He was an idiot.

"A little humiliation goes a long way. As does some apologizing and actually communicating. From what I hear, you need a little of all three."

"I thought you didn't like gossip." What had Leah heard, and where from?

"It's not gossip if Tabby told me. We're friends. When friends talk, it's conversation. It's sharing. It's what people do when they're in a relationship."

"What did she say?" Maybe this was why Tabitha was giving him a cold shoulder bigger than the iceberg that sank the Titanic.

"That you were heading to Europe after summer camp, and you asked Tabby to go with you. That you'd asked her to go against everything you both believe as Christians and go on some romantic tour through France and Italy. Just the two of you."

"That's not what I said."

She shrugged. "I figured Tabby must have misunderstood you, that you didn't suggest anything inappropriate. But you are leaving—"

"I'm not leaving. That is, I was leaving before because I got a job in France that starts the week after I finish up at camp." Before he'd fallen for Tabitha. Before he'd met Jonas. Before . . .

"And Tabby knows you're only leaving because you have a job, and that you're coming back?" Leah tapped a finger against her lips.

"That's what I told her." But was that what she'd heard? "I also told her about the job—"

"She didn't say anything about a job."

Had she misunderstood that as well?

"So what's the job?"

"Tour guide for a company that organizes walking tours through France. We basically walk the route with the paying customers and do all the admin—organize baggage transfers, allocate rooms, order meals, sort out any problems they have along the way. Basic stuff."

"Similar to the work she does at the rowing club and at the inn." Leah didn't look convinced.

"Anyway, the company told me they've had a lot more bookings than normal, so they want to have two guides on each tour —one male, one female. In our own rooms or sharing with a same-sex guest in the smaller hotels."

"Not sharing with each other."

"No way. Is that what she thought? We're Christians. I'd never suggest that."

"She thought you weren't. Wait. That's awful English." Leah closed her eyes for a second. "What I meant to say was that

Tabby didn't know you were a Christian until a few weeks ago. Easter, I think."

"Tabitha didn't know I was a Christian?" Logan hadn't expected that. Sure, he'd never come right out and told her, but it wasn't the kind of thing that had come up in conversation. "I guess that explains why she's been a little standoffish over the years."

"She's always liked you—"

She had?

"—but she wasn't going to get involved with an unbeliever."

Which made perfect sense. If anything, he respected her even more for that. "Is that why she got the wrong end of the stick? Because she was wondering if she'd been right all along, and I wasn't a Christian?"

"Maybe." Leah's tone was light, as though Logan's faith or lack thereof was exactly the reason Tabitha had misinterpreted his invitation and withdrawn from him. "But she was wrong, so now we need to get the two of you back together. What were you thinking?"

Logan leaned against the counter and shared the plan.

———

TABBY WOKE up after yet another sleepless night. It had been two weeks since book club, two weeks of sleepless nights, two weeks spent tossing and turning, going backward and forward in her mind about what Logan had said, what Granny Gracie had said, what Hannah and Leah had said. What Dad had said. What Gran would have said if she'd been here.

She'd rested. And she'd prayed—something Gran would have reminded her to do right from the get-go. She'd been so caught up in missing Gran and trying to memorialize her by renovating the boat shed that she'd forgotten the most important thing.

God didn't want her to *do*. God wanted her to *be*. To be herself. To be in His presence. To be and become the person He'd created her to be.

She'd spoken to Shelby Short, who was now working three mornings a week at the inn, cleaning the kitchen, the inn's public rooms, and the guest rooms. That gave Tabby a chance to think and pray about her choices, her dreams, and God's plan.

A couple of tough conversations with Dad and Hannah had reminded her that she did have choices and saying yes to one thing—like working for Hannah or managing the inn—meant saying no to something else—like renovating and running the boat shed or going to Europe or New Zealand with Logan.

She'd prayed about that a lot. Granny Gracie had made her views clear on traveling to New Zealand, and Leah had called in at the rowing club and made a couple of veiled comments about Europe. Even assuming the Europe trip was on the up-and-up, Tabby still wasn't ready to say yes. Some still small voice inside said *Wait*. Well, she'd wait. Her passport was valid for ten years, and Europe's historic buildings, culture, and food weren't going anywhere.

That left the boat shed. Or The Boatshed, as she was now thinking of it. The word on The Boatshed was also "wait" but for a different reason—she was still waiting for the city to consider the rezoning application. As annoying as that was for someone as results-oriented as Tabby, the waiting did at least give her time to think through the options for the building—daytime café or day and evening restaurant or irregular events venue. She'd asked God about that decision as well and gotten the same answer. *Wait*.

Well, Dad had said she needed to trust God, so she was.

God, there are a lot of options and choices in front of me. I don't yet know which path to take, so I'm going to borrow Logan's verses and add one of Gran's. I'm going to trust Your path, not my own understanding. I ask You light the path You want me to take, and make the path straight so I don't accidentally go the wrong way.

Today was Saturday. Last week's campers would all have left this morning, and the counselors and volunteers would spend the afternoon cleaning and tidying, ready for the next group to arrive tomorrow. Which made today the perfect day to visit the camp and talk to Logan.

And now it's time to find Logan and ask his forgiveness. I ask that You go before me and prepare his heart as You have mine, that You give me the words to say, and that Your will be done.

She didn't say "amen" as she knew she'd be praying a lot more between now and when she arrived at Camp Trinity.

For now, it was time to work through her regular routine of feeding and seeing off her guests, cleaning, and making up their rooms in preparation for tonight's new arrivals.

Maybe Dad and Logan were right. She'd hired help at the inn, but maybe it was also time to cut her hours at the rowing club.

If Logan forgave her.

And there was only one way to find out, which meant pulling on her big-girl boots, borrowing the car, and heading out to Lake Other and Camp Trinity.

The cooking, cleaning, and checking out went faster than she'd anticipated, and she was soon in Dad's car, heading toward camp, toward Logan. It struck her that time did not move at a constant pace—it dragged unbearably before something she'd been antici-pating, like her first date with Logan, but sped faster than light before something she was dreading. Like this conversation.

God, help me.

Maybe Logan wouldn't be there.

Maybe he wouldn't be available.

Maybe he wouldn't want to listen.

No, that was defeat talking.

And she'd arrived.

She pulled into the camp's driveway and crawled toward the parking lot at the walking pace dictated by the sign at the entrance. She passed several small log cabins scattered around the site—the camper accommodation—brick kitchen and dining rooms, and a large log meeting room. The camp was bigger than she remembered. How was she going to find Logan? He could be anywhere.

The parking lot appeared on her right, and she pulled in and parked, turned off the engine, and leaned her head against the steering wheel. *God, this is Your idea, so I'm trusting that it's going to be easy to find Logan. Amen.*

"Tabitha?"

A knock sounded on the car window, and she bolted upright. Logan. *Thank You, God.*

"Are you okay?" Logan said through the window. "What are you doing here?"

"Looking for you." As she climbed out of the car, her knees threatened to give way, and she leaned against the car for support. It had only been three weeks since she'd seen him, yet she felt like she was meeting him for the first time, with the resulting shortness of breath and inability to speak a single word, let alone string together a complete and coherent sentence. "Do you have a few minutes?"

"For you? Of course. I've missed you." Logan reached toward her, arms open, then stopped. "Can I have a hug?"

Walking into Logan's arms felt like coming home.

"So why are you here?" Logan asked, his breath tickling her ear.

"I'vecometoapologize." Tabby spoke so quickly the whole sentence came out as one word. She took a deep breath. *Here goes, God. Please give me the words to say, and Logan the heart to hear them.* "I behaved badly. I should have listened and heard you out, not frozen you out. Your challenge felt like a personal attack, as though—"

"As though I had everything all figured out—when I clearly don't—and was belittling you because you didn't."

She hadn't been going to go that far, but if he was admitting it . . . "Kind of. I reacted badly to your suggestion that I need to make some changes in my life—like reducing my workload—because it felt like you were saying my work didn't matter. Then you suggested we go traveling together and that just tipped me over the edge."

Logan hugged her a little tighter and there was a touch on the top of her head that could have been a kiss.

"Now I realize you were speaking out of concern. What I do does matter . . . but I have to choose to do the right things for the right reasons. I have to remind myself to bring God into my decisions."

"You have a servant heart. That makes it hard for you to say no to people. But sometimes you must, because what other people ask you to do might be taking you away from what God is calling you to."

"People are always asking me to help."

"You don't have to say no. Just don't say yes. The people who are asking you are Christians. They'll understand if you say you need to pray about something before giving an answer. That way you're giving yourself time to ask God and figure out if it's something He wants you to do." He released her, running his hands down her arms until he held her hands. "Let's go for a walk."

"That's a good idea." Tabby grabbed her purse and locked her car. "You suggested I come to France and Italy with you, and New Zealand. I think I misunderstood. What were you asking?"

"I've been offered a three-month job starting in August for a company that organizes walking tours in Europe. They want two guides on each tour—one male, one female—to provide extra support. We'd have separate rooms, but would work together on stuff like baggage transfers, room allocation, and meals."

Exactly what Leah had suggested.

"But that assumes I take the job," Logan said as they strolled together in the direction of the lake.

"Why wouldn't you?"

"That comes down to the answer to the bigger questions, the same questions I've been asking you. What's my dream? What's my God-given calling? And how does your calling fit with mine?" Logan stopped walking and grasped her other hand.

"You said you came to Trinity Lakes to figure out what God wanted from you. How's that going? Have you made any progress in figuring it out?"

"As it happens, I have." Logan released her and held her at arm's length. "Can I take you out for dinner tonight and tell you about it?"

"That sounds like a great idea. Where are we going?"

"Wear something nice. I'll pick you up at seven."

CHAPTER TWENTY-TWO

Tabby twirled in front of Hannah and Leah, who'd arrived only minutes after Tabby's SOS text requesting help for her impromptu date. Between them, they'd arrived with more hair and beauty products than the average beauty parlor. Hannah had sat her in front of the mirror and done her makeup.

"Hannah, where did you get all this stuff? And how do you know how to use it?" Tabby couldn't believe that Hannah, who rarely wore makeup herself, had done such an amazing job.

"I'm Susannah Gilbertson's daughter." Hannah snorted, the same unladylike snort as her grandmother. "Mother dear made sure I had a near-professional level of skill with cosmetics 'just in case' I gave up on rowing and decided to do something sensible, like enter beauty pageants."

Leah's contribution was styling Tabby's hair into some kind of fancy knot at the back of her head, then gluing it in place with what felt like a full can of heavy-duty hairspray.

"What do you think?" Leah asked.

"I feel . . . pretty." Tabby was wearing a knee-length fifties-style dress she'd found in Gran's wardrobe, heeled sandals she'd borrowed from Leah, and her whole outfit had a very *West Side Story* vibe.

"You look gorgeous." Leah gave a satisfied nod.

"Gorgeous," Hannah echoed.

"You don't think it's too much?" Hair, makeup, dress. It was all a little too fancy for Trinity Lakes.

"It's perfect." Leah and Hannah shared what could only be described as a significant look. They knew more than they were letting on.

At precisely seven o'clock, there was a knock on the inn's front door. That had to be Logan, because guests usually rang the doorbell.

"Tabby, do you want me to get that?" Dad called up the stairs.

"Yes, please." This was their first formal date, the first time Logan had picked her up, so it seemed appropriate that Dad should answer the door and give Logan the traditional paternal first-date grilling. Not that Dad would.

The front door closed, and men's voices rumbled downstairs, but her room was too far away for her to tell what they were saying.

She said goodnight to Hannah and Leah, then slipped through Gran's almost-finished suite and came to a stop at the top of the formal wooden staircase that stretched from the front entrance to the guest rooms.

Logan was wearing a smart navy suit she'd never seen before, and oh my goodness, he did fill it out nicely. Tabby held the banister as she descended the stairs, trying not to clomp in the unfamiliar heels and ruin the mood.

"Tabitha. You look amazing."

"Thank you. Nice suit." It looked even better up close.

"Thanks. It came with the car." He gestured out the door toward Caleb's truck. "Your chariot awaits. Goodnight, Mr. Thomas."

"Goodnight, Dad."

"Have fun, you two."

Tabby allowed Logan to take her hand, escort her to the truck, and open the door.

"Where are we going," she asked once they were both in the truck.

"It's a surprise."

Tabby was not a fan of surprises, and her hesitance must have shown.

"It's a good surprise. I promise. Now, can you keep your eyes closed?" He pulled a silk scarf from his pocket. "Or would you rather wear a blindfold?"

"I can keep my eyes closed."

"Good. No peeking, Tabitha." He put the car into gear and drove off as she closed her eyes.

Tabby tried to work out where they were going based on the turns Logan took, but it was impossible. The inn was close to one of the main routes out of town, and they didn't take that road—she could tell based on their speed. He didn't cross the bridge and take the south or east routes out of town either. So where were they going? He wasn't going to tell her, but they had to talk about something.

"Why do you always call me Tabitha?"

"Because that's how I see you." His tone was matter-of-fact, as though the answer was obvious.

"What do you mean?" She hadn't meant to say the words out loud.

"Tabby reminds me of a cat—sleepy and self-centered. You're the opposite—always bright and cheery, always on the go, always putting other peoples' needs before your own."

She squeezed her eyes even more tightly closed. She couldn't let tears leak out and ruin her makeup.

"You're like Tabitha in the Bible—some translations call her Dorcas. The name means 'gazelle,' and the original Tabitha was a woman abounding in good deeds and acts of charity. That's who you are. You're graceful like a gazelle, and a gracious host to me, to all your guests."

Oh.

Wow.

She blinked a few times and wiped a finger under each eye to blot the moisture.

"No peeking, remember." Now she could hear the familiar humor in his tone.

"I promise." All she'd seen was darkness all around.

Logan slowed then stopped the truck. "I'll come around and let you out."

She had no idea where they were, beyond the fact that they must still be in Trinity Lakes.

Logan's door slammed closed, hers opened, and he helped her out of the car, then closed the door behind her.

They were outside, and she was standing on what felt like gravel beneath her strappy sandals. He put his arm around her waist and led her along a short path. She was grateful for his support—between his words, the unfamiliar heels, and the stones beneath her feet, she probably wouldn't be able to walk without him beside her.

"Careful. We have a couple of steps up." He guided her up what sounded like two wooden steps and onto a wooden floor. The sound of her footsteps changed. Were they inside? If so, the room must be dim because she couldn't detect bright light from behind her closed eyelids.

"Keep your eyes closed," he said. "Just for another minute."

"Where are we?" Their voices echoed a little, as though they were in a large, empty room. The air smelled fresh and clean, with hints of garlic and candlewax.

"You'll find out in a minute. Your table awaits." He led her across a wooden floor—she could tell by the tip-tap of her heels —and let her hand go to help her into a seat.

She felt in front of herself and found a flat surface covered in fabric—a table and tablecloth? There was a click, and gentle piano music floated through the air.

Another chair scraped on the wooden floor from in front of her. Logan must be taking a seat.

"You can open your eyes now."

Tabby opened her eyes slowly, not wanting to be blinded by bright indoor lights. But the lights weren't bright like in a restaurant. Instead, she was surrounded by flickering candle-light. Even so, it took her eyes a few seconds to adjust and take in her surroundings.

She was seated at a small table lit by an assortment of tealight candles. The setting was picture perfect, like any one of the dozens of wedding settings she'd found in Gran's scrap-books—a white linen tablecloth topped by a red table runner, round red placemats, and white plates. A single red rose perched in a small vase. Instrumental music played in the background.

Tabby picked up her napkin, unfolded it and rested it across her lap as she looked past the table. She was surrounded by a dozen or more flickering church candles sitting on an old wooden floor, placing her and Logan in a candlelit oasis . . . where?

"Where are we?" There was something familiar about the room, even though most of it was bathed in darkness. The open space, the wooden floors, the slight smell of water and algae, the sound of lapping water . . .

"Are we in the boat shed?"

"Did you peek?"

"We are? That doesn't make sense. It's clean. I didn't trip over any rotting floorboards. There's a bit of a smell, but none of the stink from last time."

"I told you it could all be fixed with bleach and some elbow grease."

"But who? When? How?"

"Jasper Cohen and some of the other boys from the gym have been coming in those afternoons you've been at work."

"Wow." She pushed back from the table and stood.

"Careful," Logan stood and reached toward her. "They've fixed the broken boards between here and the door, but they haven't got to them all. I don't want you taking a tumble."

"And I'll sit right back down." Tabby wore flat shoes seven days a week and hadn't broken out the heels since Gran's funeral. She didn't want to ruin this reunion with a trip to the ER. Logan stood and moved into the shadows to her right.

"This is beautiful. She picked up a silver spoon and examined it under the candlelight. "Is this the set we found in Gran's room?"

"Yes. The tablecloths and napkins are from her room as well." Logan stood and moved over to a sideboard, where he picked up two plates.

"I'm . . . It all looks amazing."

And something smelled amazing as well.

"Voilà." He placed a plate in front of her, and the other at his place setting. "Homemade sourdough bruschetta with basil and tomato." He pointed to the left of her plate, then the right. "And prosciutto with buffalo mozzarella."

"This looks delicious."

"What would you like to drink? Sparkling apple juice—which you Americans call cider—or ginger beer?" He held up two bottles.

"Apple, please."

He poured them each a glass, sat down, took her hand, and gave thanks. "Amen."

"Amen. Where did all this come from?" Tabby asked as she lifted the tomato bruschetta and took a small bite. Hadn't he been at camp all day?

"The food is all from Leah's store, and one of the chefs from camp cooked for me."

Impressive. But . . .

"You didn't plan all this in an afternoon." He couldn't have. It wasn't possible. Which meant he'd planned it all out while she was still doubting him, still ignoring him, still ghosting him. That spoke volumes about his character.

"Once you said yes, it was just a case of getting the food prepared and delivered and adding the final touches." His airy tone suggested it was no big deal. But it was a big deal. A huge deal.

"Is that why we drove around half of Trinity Lakes while I had my eyes closed?"

"I wanted to give you an idea of what the place could be like. Imagine glass bifold doors looking out onto the lake, and full-length windows looking toward the mountains. A veranda for photographs during the day, or starlit dinners at night."

"It sounds amazing." And romantic. But nothing could be more romantic than this candlelit dinner created especially for her. "I want—need—to apologize again." The words needed to be said, particularly given Logan's spectacular surprise in putting this whole evening together. "The planning, the cleaning, the music, the food . . . it's all incredible. Especially given how our last conversation ended. I jumped to a crazy conclusion and didn't give you the opportunity to explain. I am sorry."

"Good communication is the basis of any relationship." Logan reached across the table and took her hand. "I'm sure it won't be the last time we misunderstand each other or disagree."

"I'm sure you're right."

"I'm told the trick is to get past the disagreement part and on to the kiss-and-make-up part as quickly as possible." He gave a flirty Magnum-esque lift of the eyebrows.

"Is that so?" Tabby matched his tone.

They finished their starter, and Logan rose to clear the plates to the side table. Now her eyes had adjusted to the light, she could make out some food warmers.

"For our main, Marcus has prepared baked salmon with a parmesan crust, served on parmesan risotto, with a trio of greens on the side—new season asparagus spears, green beans, and broccolini." As Logan spoke, he served each item with the flair of someone trained in silver service. One of his many short-term jobs, no doubt.

He sat back down, and they started eating.

"Have you had anymore thoughts about what you'd like to do with the building?"

"I've been praying about it, and I get the strongest feeling to wait. To take the process one step at a time and trust that the right decision will be obvious when the time comes."

"And until then?"

"I've hired a student—Shelby Short from Bella Italia—to help at the inn a few mornings a week so I can take some half-days off. It's given me time to think and pray." Tabby took a mouthful of salmon. "This is delicious."

"Have you heard any answers?"

"The same as for the building—wait. So I'm waiting." She wanted to be doing, not waiting, but she was learning—relearning—to listen for God's voice, to trust His will and not her own desire to be doing. "I've also been cooking, trying to figure out recipes for The Boatshed. Partly because the kitchen is my happy place, and partly because I'm getting frustrated with all the waiting."

"But it's not 'just' waiting, is it?" Logan tap-tapped his fingers on the tablecloth. "It's waiting and trusting. Trusting God to provide a path and following that path."

"I guess so." So what was Logan's path? "This afternoon, you said you'd made some progress in figuring out what God wanted from you."

"I think so. I was talking with one of the camp leaders, Jonas

Simmons. He's also the deputy principal at Trinity Lakes High."

"I remember Mr. Simmons." A good man.

"Jonas thinks I'd make a good high school teacher."

"You would." Teaching would fit with his background and skills, especially given what Leah's semi-legitimate cyber-stalking had uncovered. "You'd be a great teacher."

"Jonas says I can do a supervised internship at the high school and some online classes to get credentialed. It will mean staying in Trinity Lakes for at least the next year. But if you're interested in the job in France—"

"I'm not. At least, not right now. I like the idea of travel, but I wouldn't want your life—the life you've had, always living out of a suitcase. Or backpack."

"Then I'll stay. I know home is important to you."

"You'd stay in Trinity Lakes?" *For me* she wanted to ask but didn't dare.

"If there was a reason to stay. If you wanted me to stay. If you're going to stay."

If it was up to Tabby, she would ask Logan to stay with her in a fraction of a heartbeat. But it wasn't only up to her, was it? Was this what God meant by "wait"?

"Gran would have said I shouldn't change my whole life to fit in with yours. The same goes for you—you shouldn't change your life for me. Staying in Trinity, taking up teaching . . . that sounds a lot like changing your life." Tabby took a deep breath and sent up a quick prayer. *God, please give me the words*. "We both need to be sure you're changing for the right reason. For God. Not for me."

"I could say the same thing. If I decide to stay, I need to know you're staying for the right reasons—because this is where God wants you. If I left Trinity and you came too, I'd need to know you were following God's calling. Not following me." Logan set down his knife and fork and rested his hands on the edge of the table.

"If God means for us to be together, then He's not going to give us conflicting calls." Surely conflicting calls would be a sign from God that they weren't meant to be together.

"I agree." Logan propped his elbows on the table. "It also means that if our calls change, they'll change in the same direction."

"So we're going to have to trust God and believe that if He means for us to be together, He'll make it clear." *God, if I'm not meant to be with Logan, please make it clear tonight, here and now. Otherwise it's going to be too painful.*

"And trust each other, that we're not going to put personal feelings ahead of where we believe God is calling us, now and in the future."

The music changed, and Tabby recognized the tune. "Always By My Side." Not a well-known song, perhaps, but one of her favorites. She stood. "Shall we dance?"

"Why not?" Logan stood and moved to her, then took her in his arms, and they swayed in time to the music.

They were both on the same page. That was a huge relief. But now came the personal question, the tough question, the make-or-break question. "Do you think we're meant to be together?"

"I believe I'm called to stay in Trinity Lakes. For now. Not necessarily forever." Logan gave a wry smile. "I get that you'd like to know more than the next year. So would I. But that's all I've got right now."

"I understand." And she did. She believed God had a plan for her life. For their lives. But He didn't show the whole plan on a billboard for her to see. It was more like it was written in a book, and she had to discover it one page at a time.

"What about you?" Logan asked. "Do you think we're meant to be together?"

"I pray about staying or leaving, about the inn or The Boatshed, and I get the same response: wait. Home is important to me, and it's where I feel I should be right now. That doesn't mean I never want to go anywhere. It just means I need to wait."

"And in the future?"

"I pray about you, and . . ." Tabby was putting herself out on a limb, but Logan already had, and this wasn't the time to be the coy, submissive woman. "And being with you is the only thing I am sure about."

The song came to an end, and Logan came to a slow stop, pulling Tabby close and holding her hands. He looked straight into her eyes.

"Tabitha, I love you. I want to stay. I want us to be together. I want to spend life by your side. I'm not clear where God wants me or what He wants me to do in the long term. But I am clear that right now, I'm meant to be here, in Trinity Lakes. And I would love it if you were here with me."

"I love you, too, and I can't think of anything I'd like more. Being with you now. Traveling with you in the future. Being with you always."

"I don't know where the future will lead us. I don't know what God's got in store. But I know where God is leading me, where my heart is leading me." He touched his lips to hers in a kiss that was gentle and electrifying and a promise of things to come. "I want to be with you forever. Always by my side."

The End

Thank you for reading *Always By My Side.* I hope you enjoyed Tabby and Logan's story.

Reviews help other readers find books they'll enjoy reading. Please consider writing a review and sharing your thoughts with other readers on Amazon or your favorite retail site, or tell your friends in real life and on social media.

ACKNOWLEDGMENTS

Writing and publishing a novel takes the proverbial village. I have been helped along this journey by too many people to name, including Catherine Hudson, Rochelle Stephens, Rose Dee, Dorothy Adamek, Margie Lawson, Andrea Grigg, Jessica Kate, my friends at Omega Writers and Romance Writers of New Zealand, and all my editing clients over the years whose projects have helped me hone my own craft.

A huge thank you my fellow Trinity Lakes authors—Narelle Atkins, Meredith Resce, Lisa Renee, Carolyn Miller, Jenny Glazebrook, and Sara Beth Williams—for inviting me to be part of this series, for your invaluable feedback on my draft manuscript, and for your unfailing support and advice as I write, edit, and publish. This has truly been a collaborative process, and I thank God for you all.

Also, thank you to my newsletter subscribers for rising to the challenge and helping me name several minor characters: Christabelle Allestad, Carol Ashby, Narelle Atkins, Deborah Boyd, Susan Branch, and Caroline Cook.

Thanks also to Lesley Ann McDaniel, who edited my manuscript and pointed out all those pesky typos and continuity errors, as well as challenging me to go deeper.

Thanks to my husband for encouraging me to go to that first writing conference, for supporting my long writing apprenticeship, and for disappearing for long enough for me to get this finished on time.

Finally, thanks to God, who grants us the desires of our hearts, for the endless "God-incidences" that have taken me from avid reader to aspiring writer to published author.

To God be the glory.

Psalm 37:4

ABOUT THE AUTHOR

Iola Goulton writes contemporary Christian romance with a Kiwi connection. "Iola" is a Welsh name which means "valued by the Lord," and it's pronounced "yo-la" (not eye-ola).

Iola is the empty-nest mother of two who lives with her husband in the sunny Bay of Plenty, New Zealand, not far from Hobbiton. Yes, Hobbiton is a real place. She works part-time as a freelance editor and part-time for a local company, wrangling spreadsheets by day and words by night.

Visit iolagoulton.com to find out more about Iola, and to sign up for her author newsletter.

www.ingramcontent.com/pod-product-compliance
Lightning Source LLC
Chambersburg PA
CBHW030936210726
48290CB00007B/2216